Con

CW00557062

Join Our Readers' Group	v
Monster's Temptation Soundtrack	ix
Monster and Me	xi
Prologue	1
Chapter 1	15
Chapter 2	30
Chapter 3	41
Chapter 4	49
Chapter 5	60
Chapter 6	73
Chapter 7	83
Chapter 8	105
Chapter 9	117
Chapter 10	129
Chapter 11	141
Chapter 12	154
Chapter 13	164
Chapter 14	174
Chapter 15	193
Chapter 16	204
Monster's Obsession	207
Author's Note	209
Wild Moon	211
Books by C.R. Jane	223
Books By Mila Young	227
About C.R. Jane	231
About Mila Young	233

Join Our Readers' Group

Stay up to date with C.R. Jane by joining her Facebook readers' group, C.R.'s Fated Realm. Ask questions, get first looks at new books/series, and have fun with other book lovers!

www.facebook.com/groups/C.R.FatedRealm

Join Mila Young's Wicked Readers Group to chat directly with Mila and other readers about her books, enter giveaways, and generally just have loads of fun!

www.facebook.com/groups/milayoungwickedreaders

Dedication

For all of us who don't want Prince Charming.

*We'd rather sleep with the Monsters because they know better
than anyone exactly how to make us scream...*

The Monster
Eminem & Rihanna

Monster
Kanye West & Others

Monsters
All Time Love & blackbear

Monster
Skillet

I Fell In Love With The Devil
Avril Lavigne

Here Come The Monsters
ADONA

Noise Is Gone
Ludovico Technique

Diabolic Crush
Third Realm

The Sound of Silence
Disturbed

Listen to the Spotify Playlist at https://spoti.fi/3tJLC44

Monster and Me

From C.R. Jane and Mila Young

Monster's Temptation

The Monster King wants to play...

It's been 1097 days and 14 hours since I've been locked in this place.

And they've come to me every night.

The monsters in my dreams worship my body.

And when I wake up, I'm desperate for more...

But they're never there to finish me off.

Dr. Adams says I can leave the asylum if I start to take my meds, but I've always hated how they made me feel...and I'm not sure that I agree with them that I'm actually crazy.

Because dreams don't make you crazy, right?

I've got to start living someday though...so I finally take the plunge and obey so I can get out.

My dreams stop, and the monsters disappear. I'm finally starting a new life.

And that's when he comes...the monster king.

Evidently my little dreams, weren't just dreams. And he and his demon horde were feeding off my lust.

Their glowing eyes, sharp teeth, and big...

They're all real.

The Monster King wants me back. I'm their favorite plaything after all.

And I just might want to play.

Monster's Temptation is book 1 in this deliciously monstrous duet.

Prologue

Blake

A girl should really get some kind of warning when her life's about to go to hell.

But I hadn't.

There wasn't a single warning that by the end of that day, everything was going to be over.

THE ALARM on my phone dragged me from a restless sleep, and after turning it off, I just laid there, staring up at the ceiling. Another day.

Awesome.

Maybe most girls would have seen my life from the outside and thought I was completely out of my fucking mind that I was so miserable all the time. But you had to grow up inside the belly of the beast to really understand. The Governor's Mansion glittered from the outside, but inside, it was rotting.

Or at least that's what it felt like every fucking day. I was just counting down the days until I left for college. Stanford was calling my name. The college was far enough away while still being acceptable in pedigree to my parents.

I could almost taste my freedom.

Reluctantly, I rolled out of bed, knowing that Annie, one of the staff who'd been assigned to me, would be by any minute to check I was on schedule.

I washed my face and put on my freshly pressed navy and burgundy uniform, and then I carefully curled my hair and applied a light layer of makeup.

Looking in the mirror, I wondered if there would be a point where I would recognize the girl staring back at me. Long, shiny black hair that was so long it almost fell to my ass...much to my mother's chagrin. Blue eyes that I always got compliments on, and lips that were too big for my face. I was decent looking; I'd never been insecure about that. But the girl in the mirror had no backbone. She was told to jump, and she did.

I hated her.

My stomach clenched as a sharp, stabbing pain darted through it. I leaned over and clenched my teeth as my vision swam and a wave of nausea hit me. Fuck.

A knock on the door sounded behind me and I took a deep breath, knowing it wasn't an option to try for a sick day, not when I had a test today that my parents knew about.

I straightened up and took a few deep breaths. Two more months and I'd be free.

"Come in," I called, when I'd gotten my shit together enough I could ensure that my voice sounded normal.

"You're ten minutes behind schedule," Annie chided gently as she peeked in through the door.

I nodded and forced a smile.

"Put on some more blush. You're looking a bit pale," she instructed, her gaze moving over me as it did every morning, making sure that I looked perfect before the Governor saw me.

I did as she asked and then followed her out into the hall-way, my heels sinking into the plush crimson carpet as I walked. It was kind of creepy living in such a perfectly preserved piece of history. Sometimes I swore that the people in the black and white photographs on the wall were watching me as I passed. After living in this decadent mausoleum, I was determined that any place I called home in the future was going to be brand new and modern-looking. I'd had enough of living in the past to last me a lifetime.

I heard the soft clink of glassware as we approached the dining room. Because our family couldn't be anything but fancy, we couldn't eat in the kitchen at the small, round table in there. Instead, we had to eat at the long, ornate table that could feed thirty. It made every morning so cozy.

As usual, my parents were seated at the table. My father was reading his daily reports while my mother gossiped about some politician's wife. I could understand why her hair always looked so volumetric; she knew secrets about what seemed like every fucking person in this state. The secrets had to stay somewhere.

Neither of them paid me any attention as I walked into the room, but I was used to that. I settled into the shiny wooden seat that was about as uncomfortable as sitting on a pin cushion, and I placed my napkin in my lap. Like a well-oiled machine, one of the kitchen staff came hustling forward with my plate practically the moment the napkin was moved.

"Kayla, take that roll straight back to the kitchen," my mother snapped after the lid to my plate had been taken off, revealing a delicious smelling omelette and a croissant. "And is that cheese on that omelette? I believe I specifically told you all that she needed to be watching her weight. It's like none of you have a brain cell."

"Miranda," my father said mildly, not taking his eyes off

the paper he was holding. My mother shifted in her seat and took a deep breath as she struggled to tamp down her anger.

"She." That's pretty much all I was to my mother. I think I heard her say the servant's names about ten times more than she ever said mine. Or "the girl." That was another title my mother loved to throw around when she was referencing me.

"Don't worry, Mother. I'll eat around the cheese," I drawled insolently, and her lips pinched. I knew she was just itching to slap me in the face for my tone, but at least around the staff...and before school, she wasn't going to do anything.

Pain ricocheted through my stomach again, and the fork I'd been holding clattered to my plate.

That did get my father's attention. "What the fuck is wrong with you?" he barked.

"Nothing," I answered through clenched teeth as I picked the fork back up with a shaking hand. My father eyed me closer, just daring me to do something else, but when I placed a bite of egg into my mouth without doing anything out of the ordinary, his attention went back to his report.

It was the only bite of breakfast that I managed to get down. I spent the next fifteen minutes just cutting my food into small pieces and pretending to put things in my mouth so it looked like some of the food was disappearing. You'd think that my mother would love to see me not eating, but she was the kind of woman who could never be pleased. I was either eating too much, or I had an eating disorder. There was no in-between.

My father finally set down his fork and stood up, my mother quickly following. They left the room without a word to me, and I breathed a sigh of relief as I put down my own fork and struggled not to be sick.

I just need to get through my test, I thought to myself as I shakily stood up. I walked out of the room and headed towards the front door where one of the staff was standing, holding my bookbag and the lunch that would've been prepared for me, because heaven forbid the Governor's daughter be seen standing in the lunch line.

Tony, our main driver, was standing in front of one of our family's many black town cars right out front in the circle driveway that extended in front of the mansion. I got into the car and endured my usual silent ride to school.

It said a lot for my home life that Winthrop Academy was a reprieve. Because the people there, they were awful. Putting together a bunch of pampered superstars in one place was a quick way to ensure that your classmates would be assholes.

We pulled up to the front of the school, the dark red brick and Corinthian columns covered in ivy an instant giveaway that this was an elite institution. Everything about Winthrop was meant to set you up for success. It was one of the school's principles, in fact, that you should constantly be preparing for success. Which meant that everything about Winthrop was designed to mimic the Ivy League institutions that we would be attending in the future.

Or Stanford...if I had my way at all.

I didn't bother saying goodbye to Tony. He'd been instructed by my parents to not talk to me unless it was absolutely necessary, but he did give me a slight wink as I left. Or that could have been an eye twitch...or a tic. Sometimes I just liked to imagine that the staff liked me.

I walked up the golden brick-paved path that led up to the imposing wooden doors of the entrance that were currently open to allow students to pass through. There were giant lion heads carved into the middle of the doors with brass loops hanging down. Except they were so far up the door that you'd have to be a giant in order to actually use them as a door knocker. I'm sure that the doors were meant to be some kind of symbol, but I'd never cared enough to find out.

I was sweating as I walked down the hallway teeming with

5

uniformed students. No one talked to me, but I knew that everyone was very much aware of my presence.

You would think that everyone would be trying to kiss my ass here since my father was the most powerful man in the state, and a sure contender for the presidency after his term of governor was over. But instead of breeding ass-kissing worshipers, my father's fame had bred assholes.

The things my classmates did to torture me were always done on the sly; they didn't want to run the risk of getting in trouble, after all. It didn't matter though, they all seemed to be experts in subterfuge. I would be tripped while walking down a row in between desks, and everyone would act innocent. My uniform was stolen from my gym locker and cut into a million pieces so I had to borrow the school's castoffs. I had to suffer everything silently because heaven forbid I told my parents that I had a problem at school. They would consider it a personal attack on them that I couldn't manage to charm the sheep they so easily kept in place.

Last week in the cafeteria, one of the scholarship students had been tripped right as he was walking past me, and he'd dumped his pasta all over the top of my head.

On and on it went for the last four years...but still, it wasn't as bad as things were at home.

Normally I would be trying to hustle through the hallways, my head held high like nothing they did affected me. But today I was too sick to do anything but trudge. Everything was spinning a bit around me, and my stomach pain had gone past the point of nausea into full-on "I might die" kind of pain.

Luckily for me, my test was in second period. And although I wasn't sure that I would be able to even read the math problems on my test, at least I could go to the nurse's office right afterwards.

I'd almost made it to my classroom when I was suddenly

pulled into someone's hard chest and familiar cold fish lips slid against mine.

I gagged when a slimy tongue slid into my mouth and attempted to tangle with mine.

I ripped my head backwards, but not with the force that I usually put in when confronted with Adam Simmons' antics. Son of one of the state senators, Adam thought he was a gift from God, and my parents had emphatically pushed me in his direction every chance they got. Adam had gotten the impression I was his girlfriend, despite the fact that I informed him daily how mistaken he was.

Somehow he seemed to forget that every day. Case in point: his hands were still wrapped around my waist.

To the rest of the world, Adam would've been quite the catch. Curly blonde hair and brown sparkling eyes, he was the captain of the football team and a million girls were desperate to let him in their pants. And they did let him in their pants. He must have fucked almost every girl in this school.

It was always amazing to me how Adam had no problem telling me he was in love with me, and then was fucking a cheerleader in the football locker rooms by the end of the day.

Sometimes I found a little bit of patience for him because at least when he was standing next to me, people behaved. It was nice not to have to worry about having my hair cut, or my bra snapped, or having ketchup thrown over my clothes.

Today though, I was too sick to have any patience. I wiggled out of his grip, almost falling to the ground as I did so, and then I quickly darted into my classroom, trying not to faint.

JUST AS I SUSPECTED, the numbers on my test paper might as well have been a foreign language when I sat down to take it in second period.

But by that time, I was so sick that I didn't care.

I'd only made it halfway through the test when I knew I couldn't wait any longer. I shot out of my desk and staggered towards the door, ignoring the teacher's shout from behind me. I somehow made it down the hall into the bathroom, and then I threw up, over and over again until my nose and throat were burning and my eyes were watering.

"Ugh," I moaned as I slid onto the floor, too sick to care about how disgusting it probably was. I laid there for a good half hour before I struggled to my feet and made my way down the hallway to the nurse's office.

"Oh dear," the nurse said as soon as I walked through the door. "Come lie down."

I moaned as I got to the cot and collapsed.

The nurse came over with a thermometer and held it against my forehead. She clicked her tongue when she read the temperature. "104. You need to go home right now, young lady. Should I call your..." She hesitated, because you couldn't really just call the Governor and ask to speak with him now, could you?

"I'll just have our driver come and get me," I murmured weakly, before leaning my head over the side of the cot and throwing up all over the floor, splatters of vomit going all over the room.

Tony must have caught the urgency in my text message because he didn't ask any questions when I asked him to come pick me up, or maybe he could just tell how sick I was because of all the misspelled words. When I got the text that he'd arrived, I stumbled out of the nurse's office and made my way outside, somehow managing to make it to the car without fucking dying.

"Your parents are going to freak out," Tony grimaced as I collapsed onto the leather seat. Oh, good. He thought that right now was the best time for us to finally have a conversation. I just waved my hand at him feebly, not even sure what I was trying to convey, and he took off without another word.

As we approached the front gates that led on to the mansion's grounds, I asked him to pull around to the garage. It would be nice if I didn't have to explain why I was home to anyone, even though neither of my parents would be there. They were both machine-like in their devotion to schedules and habits. My mother would be out at the club drinking cocktails and schmoozing with her friends before her tennis lesson, while my dad would be at the Capitol Building, wheeling and dealing as he was so good at doing.

And yes, I did think it was weird that my mother got toasted before she went and played tennis.

Tony sighed and shook his head, but he listened to my request, and soon we were in the enormous nine-car garage that held my father's prized possessions—his decadent car collection.

I didn't wait for Tony to come and open the door, I was desperate to get inside and lay down before I fainted. The house was silent as I stepped inside, but I still did my best to walk as quietly as I could on the marble floors as I made my way down the hall. The main obstacle of my journey was that I had to pass my father's home office on the way to my bedroom. And although he wouldn't be home, there were always members of his staff in and out of our house, and I'm sure they would relish being able to tell on me.

I'd learned early on that my father only employed weaker versions of himself as far as his governor work went.

And weak men were snitches.

I was a few feet away from my father's office when I began to hear strange noises.

They sounded like...was someone watching porn in my father's office? And why the fuck would they leave the door cracked if they were?

Frowning, I crept towards the door, peeked inside, and saw...a fucked up scene that I couldn't have imagined in my wildest dreams.

My father...on all fours on the floor by his desk, his chief of staff Ryan—a man—fucking him in the ass while our gardener, Dale, sucked his dick from underneath.

Oh, and let's not forget the fact that his secretary, Stacey, was sprawled out in front of him, moaning like a porn star while he ate her out. I watched in shocked horror at the orgy I was seeing, bile filling my mouth.

My father moaned loudly as Dale slid his lips off his dick just in time for him to cover Dale's face with white ropes of cum, and I jumped, one of my books clattering to the floor.

They all froze, and I backed away from the door in horror.

"See who's out there," I heard my father bark. I picked up the book, stuffed it into my bag, and raced as fast as I could back in the direction that I'd come from, not wanting to lead them towards my room where they'd immediately know it was me. If I could just hide somewhere in the house...or outside...

There were a million holes in my plan, obviously—like the fact that Tony most likely had sent a text alerting my parents I was home so he didn't get chewed out later on. But it didn't matter, I had to try to escape notice.

It didn't matter that I felt like I was dying. I was pretty sure that if I was caught, I literally would die. Because he was going to kill me.

My father didn't trust me on his best day, and with a secret like this...a secret that would ruin him...

Fuck.

I turned the corner, and ran right into something—or should I say someone.

It was Ryan. Fuck.

Well, this just confirmed there was a secret fucking passage in my father's office.

I tried to pull away from him but his fingers wrapped around my arms, squeezing me so tightly I winced in pain.

Ryan hastily threw his suit pants back on, but they were unbuttoned...and he was still hard, and as he pulled me against him, his dick rubbed against me.

"Looks like someone's been a bad little girl," he whispered cruelly, and I tried to stop the tears, but I couldn't help it as I heard the slow, steady footsteps that I'd always associated with my father.

Ryan grinned down at me before whirling me around, making sure to press against my ass as he held me in place while we watched my father approach.

My father was back in his suit, the flush to his cheeks and his disheveled hair the only sign of what he'd just been partaking in.

"I won't say anything," I rushed out, knowing it was no use trying to pretend I hadn't seen him.

My father didn't say anything, he just kept walking towards me at that slow, methodical pace. As he got closer, I noticed a white streak smeared under his nose.

Oh, good, he'd been sampling some coke before his little fuck fest.

"Blake, I never wanted this to happen."

"Wanted what to happen?" I asked hoarsely.

"But I'm afraid you've forced my hand," he continued as if I hadn't said anything.

"I swear. I won't say anything!"

"I have no intention of a little bitch like you ever having something to hold over me," he said calmly. "But what are we going to do with you?"

I tried to yank away from Ryan's grip, but he was holding on too tightly.

So instead, I threw up...again.

Ryan cursed, and I tried to dart forward as his grip momentarily loosened, but Dale appeared out of nowhere, grabbing onto my hair before I'd made it any further than a few steps. White-hot pain sparked through my scalp as he yanked me backwards.

My shoulders slumped as my father stepped in front of me.

"I'd always warned you against stepping out of line, Blake," he said calmly as tears slid down my cheeks.

I didn't bother telling him how sick I was. I didn't bother begging him anymore.

I was fucked no matter what I did.

In my peripheral vision, I saw Ryan raising his hand towards me, and then something stabbed me in the neck.

"Wha—" I screeched, but the word came out funny. And when had my father turned blue? Were those black crows flying in from the windows?

I screamed as black goo began to ooze from his eyeballs.

The world began to spin around me, ghastly shapes and creatures filling my vision until I was sure the whole world had just ended.

And through it all, my father's dark chuckle was like a violent soundtrack, signaling the end of my world.

TURNED out the right dose of untraceable hallucinogens could make it very easy to persuade doctors that you'd gone crazy. And it turned out when you were the governor of the state it was no problem to convince a judge to grant a conservatorship so that you were completely under your father's control no matter what age you were. It also turned out that the best place to make sure a person disappeared without killing them was an insane asylum.

That's how I became the newest resident of Bright Meadows Asylum.

And that's how I actually became insane.

Chapter 1

Blake

"**D**on't you dare cover up, Pet," he growled as he pulled on my dress. My breath was coming out in gasps as my eyes moved across his muscled chest. He was wearing tight black pants, and I watched as he slowly slid them down his sculpted thighs, revealing a huge red dick with two heads that were designed to give me as much pleasure as possible. As I watched, his clawed hand circled his thick base, and he bit his bottom lip with a half-lidded gaze, his sharp fangs peeking out over his full lips. He was mostly human looking with the exception of a few key parts... And I'd never seen anything hotter.

"Slide those panties down so I can make you come."

I had no choice but to obey. As usual, he had me soaked and ready even though he hadn't so much as touched my skin yet. I slid down my panties obediently, and he grabbed me, pulling me into his lap and rubbing my soaking wet core over his hard length.

"Fuck, you're sexy." He yanked me forward, and my hands

automatically moved to his broad shoulders for balance as he moved me into place—my legs spread wide straddling him, my breasts flush with his chest, his huge cock flexing under me.

Despite the fact that he towered over me, in this position we were eye to eye. He was beautiful, my monster. His glowing red eyes flecked with gold sparks, his chiseled nose, his sculpted mouth that would've made Michelangelo weep. I loved the hunger in his gaze. After an entire life of never being wanted, I couldn't get enough of him...and his friends.

His lips crashed against mine in a deep kiss, and I instinctively opened my mouth, allowing his forked tongue to slide in and tangle with mine. He devoured me. His licks were aggressive and filthy, and I could feel it all the way to my core.

There was an ache inside of me that I knew only he could fill. I moaned as I returned his kiss eagerly. My hands moved from his shoulders, up his face, until I was fisting his two long black horns. I held onto them as I moved, trying to get friction on my aching clit. I was mindless with desire.

But my king wasn't in a hurry, and instead of giving me what I wanted, he simply deepened the kiss, sliding his fingers through my hair so he could hold me in place as he continued his hot, wet licks in my mouth. His other hand softly stroked my lower back, the sharp tips of his claws teasing my skin.

Tension was building inside of me, and I knew from experience that I could come just from this. His hands on my back slid down, and he squeezed my ass before grabbing his dick and positioning it right where I wanted.

"You gonna give me what I want?" he growled, and all I could do was whimper in response as he pulled me down and pushed into me. I gasped at the tight stretch. He was so big, the two heads of his crown massaging different places inside of me.

"Fuck," he groaned, a guttural growl laced in his words. "Relax, Pet. You're going to be my good girl, aren't you?" he purred.

A soft scream slipped out of me as my thighs moved flush against his and he slid all the way in. My breath came out in gasps as I tried to get a hold of myself. I was so full, it was hard to think outside of the sensations.

"Good fucking girl," he rumbled as he moved both hands to my hips and lifted me up slightly before thrusting up hard.

I whimpered again, and his grip tightened at the sound. He started fucking me desperately, his movements rough and powerful, and all I could do was go along for the ride.

His cut abdomen bunched as he moved his hips, and his gaze was hungry and determined as he watched me closely.

One of his hands moved off my hip, and he sliced down the center of my dress with his claws, showcasing my straining breasts.

He began to suckle on one of my nipples, and I gasped as my body arched backwards.

"Yes," I breathed, caught in the sensation of his mouth torturing my nipple and his long, thick cock spearing in and out of me. I continued to hold onto his long horns as we moved desperately together. His sharp fangs pricked against my skin, setting me off in an agonizingly good orgasm that threatened to destroy me.

Something slid softly against my ass, and I gasped as I peeked backwards only to see nothing visible there. But something *was sliding in between my cheeks and caressing my rosebud softly.*

"Tightest fucking pussy I've ever felt," he growled as he moved to my other nipple, his hips thrusting desperately against mine.

"Going to keep you forever, Pet. My good girl," he breathed as he stretched me.

And then...

I woke with a gasp, sweaty, and with my core aching as my

breath left me in gasps. My whole body was a live wire, and I was on the edge of orgasm; one touch and I'd go off.

Just like every morning, I had to center myself and force my brain to start working again after a night of...dreams.

Not nightmares. Obviously. They made me feel way too good for it to be that.

Although it was always a monster ravishing my body.

I peeked up at the camera situated in the wall in front of me, the red light signaling that someone on the other end was watching me. Always watching me.

I'm sure they were getting off to the sight of me panting in my sleep, my nipples peeking out from my thin pajamas. At least I hadn't woken up with my hands rubbing furiously at my core. That happened quite a bit.

Although, at least those times my body had cum before I'd woken up. Now that I was awake, it was going to be hours before my body would settle down and I wouldn't be desperate for...a dick.

I fell back into my pillow, wanting to scream. It was this place. It was what was making me go crazy.

It had started slowly. A few dreams here and there of sexy scenes with...well, the psychiatrist here actually, but then one night it had morphed.

And *they* had begun to fill my dreams.

Every night, no matter what I tried, or how much I tried to stay awake, I was sucked into an erotic dreamscape. A dreamscape where...monsters ravaged my body over and over again.

It was the same four monsters. At this point, they really did feel like my lovers because I could tell you about every one of their features. I also could describe in detail all of their weird dicks. And all the ways they liked to play.

Considering I was definitely still a virgin, these dreams were quite alarming—and uncomfortable, and they'd only ratcheted up in intensity as the months and years had gone by. Last night's dream was relatively tame; I'd been gang banged the night before. A human looking monster in my ass and pussy as I gave blow jobs back and forth to the other two.

I shifted uncomfortably in my bed as my core clenched again, begging to have some fucking relief.

If it weren't for the cameras, I would have. But with someone always watching...

My father had convinced everyone that I was crazy, and the sex dreams, the ones where my moans and screams of desire were so loud they rattled down the entire hallway...they were what cemented it.

There was no hiding what I dreamed about every night.

I'd tried the sleeping pills the doctors had given me, but those only trapped me in the dreams longer...much to the delight of Bright Meadows' other residents. Who needed porn when you had a soundtrack starring me, right?

So I didn't use the sleeping pills anymore.

The other medicine they tried to give me zombified me. The one time I'd taken them, a whole day had passed and I'd been mauled by another of the patients here, unable to do anything. I'd come to life in my room, the moon peeking through the tiny window above my head, terrified when I couldn't recall anything.

I'd refused to take the pills after that. No way was I going to be comatose at a place like Bright Meadows, where anything could happen to you.

And at least my screams weren't the scary kind. Not like all the other screams you heard in this place at night.

The screams from the other residents were always worse at night. Before I inevitably was dragged into my dreams, I would lay on my tiny cot that I was pretty sure was made of card-board, staring up at the ceiling, and then the screams would start. It was much quieter during the day, but at night it was a cruel symphony. Maybe all the patients here found it impossible to sit with their thoughts at night too.

It's not like we were tired from the day's activities. Mealtimes, medicine time, group therapy, and art therapy—they weren't exactly activities that required a lot of energy. Maybe for some people, it would've been exhausting to share their feelings, but I'd stopped sharing any of my real emotions the first week.

Since my father had threatened to kill me if I ever opened my mouth, there wasn't much that I could say except that I wasn't crazy. And apparently, that sort of thing was frowned upon in this institution. Who would've thought?

Unlike the asylums you saw in movies, the rooms in this place weren't perfectly white; instead, they were black, which felt suffocating when you could walk across the room in two steps, and your window was only as big as your head. Mornings began with a bell that sounded more like a shrill siren. It woke us up at the same time every morning at seven a.m. Evidently, they were big believers in that adage, 'rise early and go to sleep early', because I now had the sleeping hours of an 80-year-old woman.

The bell rang just then, and I sighed as I dragged myself out of bed and went to change. You were expected to switch from your dishwater gray sleeping uniform to your dishwater gray day uniform in the minutes after the bell rang. There were no mirrors in the room, and the brushes they gave you were soft and completely ineffective so you didn't try and off yourself with them, thus everyone looked like a mess all day, every day.

If you weren't out of your room within ten minutes, one of the staff would barge in and force you out. I'd had that happen once, and I'd never let it happen again. Andrew, one of the resident assholes of the institution, had made sure to do a boob and an ass grab as he yanked me out of the room, so I'd learned quickly.

After dressing, I made my way out of the living room, along with most of the others that had rooms around me. We all walked slowly to the dining area filled with circle tables to facilitate a sense of "community", where we would be served a sugar-free, gluten-free, dairy-free breakfast that basically tasted like sawdust and paint thinner, but was apparently good for our brains.

There was one prisoner—I mean patient, who sat across from me every day, and today was no different. He must have felt the same way about the breakfast as I did, because every day he would use his fingers to smear it across his entire face. It didn't matter what they gave him. Seeing him try and slather himself with vegan bacon had been a particularly interesting experience.

Props to him for livening up the place. Even if he did it with drool dripping down from his mouth.

After breakfast, we were shuffled to the nurse's station, where they forced pills down our throats and stuck their fingers in our mouths to make sure the pills were gone. Luckily I was just on a mood stabilizer after I'd refused the other pill–not that I had anything against taking medicine for mental health. But considering I didn't have any of the disorders I'd been diagnosed with while under the influence of the drug I'd been injected with on that fateful day, taking anything stronger probably wouldn't have been great.

Evidently, my father was fearful of the effect that stronger meds could have on me and had ordered that I not be given any. He recognized that stronger drugs might have the detrimental effect of "loosening" my tongue, and he wouldn't want that.

Not that anyone was ever going to believe my story. It was so outlandish that I would sound crazy to anyone who heard it. That was the beauty of my father's plan. Have everyone on the outside doubt my sanity, and everyone on the inside doubt it as well. I would never have anyone believe me again.

We had an "A" schedule and a "B" schedule, just like school, and our routine was followed strictly. Except, instead of Calculus and English, we were learning how to paint our feelings, use recorders to "play our emotions out", and talk in small groups.

That was one of the hardest things about my new reality. Not only had I been thrown in here before the end of school, but I wasn't even allowed to take any tests to get my diploma, or even a GED, despite the fact that I'd been number two in my entire class. Stanford seemed like a fantasy that I'd made up in my mind at this point.

Most of the therapists were completely intolerable. They treated us more like toddlers than adults, and I cringed every time they spoke to me in their slow, sympathetic voices.

Since I knew I didn't have a chance to get out, and the therapists weren't interested in hearing about my innocence, I'd begun telling fairy tales during group therapy. But I'd make them so convoluted that it would take at least ten minutes for the therapist to figure out what story I was telling. It was a game I played, with only myself, of course, to see how long I could go before they caught on.

Anything to make the day go by quicker.

There was only one bright spot in Bright Meadows Asylum. Steele Adams.

Dr. Steele Adams, I should say.

Seeing him twice a week was most likely the only thing that kept me from falling off the deep end and becoming as crazy as my parents claimed I was.

Dr. Adams was the most beautiful man I'd ever seen. He looked like he'd just stepped off the catwalk, and he was completely out of place in the drab, gross atmosphere I existed in now. During our sessions, I honestly wasn't even sure what we talked about, because I would get lost just looking at him and listening to the cadence of his voice. It's like someone out there had scooped out any fantasies of male attractiveness I had lurking in my brain and created him just for me.

When I was in sixth grade, I'd been to Iceland and we'd visited the Blue Lagoon. That's what his eyes reminded me of —they were a glowing blue color I'd never seen on another human being. Combined with his raven-colored hair, the effect was stunning. It was no wonder I was having dreams about him.

It was a Thursday today, which meant that I would be seeing him after breakfast.

I was pushed out of my lustful daydream by a tray clattering to the floor nearby. I looked over and saw that Candace was brandishing her spoon at a girl I'd never seen before. The poor girl was covered in the sweet potatoes the kitchen staff was trying to pass off as breakfast, and there were big tears rolling down her cheeks.

Maybe in another life, I would've stepped up to defend her since I was pretty sure that Candace was one of the resident murderers in this place. But apathy...and self-preservation was about all I was capable of feeling right now. Plus, I had a scar on my leg where Candace had somehow whittled a spoon into a knife and stabbed me in the leg a year ago. I'd bled so much that I'd passed out.

So someone else could handle Candace.

Candace started cackling wildly as orderlies rushed in. As soon as they got to her, she began to flail her arms, hitting and scratching every person that she could. "I'll kill all of you mother truckers," she screeched, making the word 'trucker' much more menacing than you would think. For some reason, Candace had a thing against swearing. She didn't care about murdering and mutilating people, but swearing crossed the line of her moral compass. "Let go of me, you butt munchers!"

She managed to cut one of the nurse's cheeks with her spoon before someone plunged a needle into her neck.

Almost immediately, her eyes took on that glazed, faraway look I was used to seeing here, and she stopped struggling. Two of the orderlies led her out of the room and then we were all instructed to go back to eating like nothing had happened. Just a typical day in Bright Meadows.

I wished I could say that Candace was the worst resident in this place, but there were far scarier people than her. And a bunch of them at that. I did my best to try and stay away from them. But every couple of months I'd slip up, and I'd be caught somewhere where the staff wasn't present. Slammed against the wall, a piece of my hair hacked off, burned with a lighter they'd come across...they were always quite inventive.

The only time that I could let my guard down was about to happen. My session with Steele.

I put my tray down, keeping my head tucked just in case any of the psychos thought I was looking at them wrong, and then hustled out of the dining area towards his office.

Butterflies ricocheted through my veins the closer I got to his door.

My dreams might've been filled with him, but he'd never given me any notion he felt similarly.

But then again, why would he? Here I was, a 21-year-old locked away in an insane asylum, while he was an accomplished doctor, able to live his life out in the real world. I wondered if he had a girlfriend out there. I didn't think he had a wife. He didn't wear a ring; not that his lack of one really meant anything.

I knocked on the door of his office, and a minute later, he opened it, a warm smile on his beautiful, beautiful lips.

"Hi," I murmured, inwardly wincing as I realized how breathy my voice sounded.

"Blake," he said with a nod, a piece of his hair falling into his face. I bit my lip in an effort to prevent myself from being weird and reaching out and brushing the curl out of his face. I'm sure that would go over well.

He was dressed in his typical uniform—a perfectly pressed, buttoned-up white collared shirt and navy black dress pants— and looked like he was about to conquer a corporate board-room instead of spending an hour asking me how I was feeling.

I passed by him with a nod and entered the room, and he followed me inside. In my daydreams—not my night dreams, since those were solely filled with creatures—he was checking out my ass as I walked right now. But our uniform pants were shapeless, so that probably wouldn't happen even if he was interested in me like that.

The room was cozy. He'd obviously done his best to make it feel welcoming. It had to have been him who decorated the place because there was no way that anyone else in Bright Meadows would care about something like comfort. There were tall shelves on every wall stuffed full of books. Most of them were boring psychology books, but there were some clas-sics scattered in there as well. He had his patients sit on a comfortable leather couch that had an assortment of squishy pillows and throw blankets he encouraged me to use every time. There was a red and black oriental rug on the floor, potted plants here and there, and a massive fireplace on the far wall that he had lit most days. Which was heaven since Bright Meadows believed that its residents should feel like human popsicles judging by the freezing temperatures we were kept in.

I settled into the couch, immediately grabbing a fuzzy blanket and wrapping it around me. Dr. Adams walked over to the fireplace and threw another log in before opening his small fridge that sat next to it and pulling out a can of my favorite orange soda.

My mouth started watering just looking at it, and it was honestly all I could do to not jump up and grab it out of his hands like I was Gollum from Lord of the Rings. *My Precious*, my inner voice cooed.

That was creepy.

"You obviously were listening last week," I said with a blush as he handed me the drink.

He smiled at me, and the butterflies in my stomach started doing freaking cartwheels and flips like they'd made it to the Olympics.

"I always listen to you," he murmured as he settled into the warm armchair across from the couch. "It just took a minute to track it down. Evidently, they stopped making it last year."

While I was definitely twitter-pated...and interested in the fact that he'd tracked down the soda I'd mentioned was my favorite, I was also thinking that I'd been trapped in here long enough that they discontinued my favorite drink. I mean, I may have been the only person in the world who drank it, so that was probably why, but it still represented the stark passage of time and all that I'd lost.

"I made you upset," he commented, leaning forward in dismay. I threw him a tremulous smile and popped the tab on my drink before taking a large gulp of the drink, moaning a bit as the fizzy orange beverage hit my tastebuds.

"Finally, something that doesn't taste like old leather," I said as I glanced at him, almost spitting my drink out when I saw the expression on his face.

He looked—almost hungry. Starving, in fact.

For me.

Dr. Adams blinked and the look disappeared. His face was blank again, only the kind, caring psychiatrist to be found.

But I swore that I'd seen it.

Unless the dreams were driving me to see sexual desire everywhere.

I didn't think that was happening. I hadn't thought Mr. Drools-a-lot was into me at lunch.

Focus, I chastised myself as I took another sip of my drink.

"So, have you thought at all about what we talked about last session?" he asked, his bright blue eyes boring into me.

I shifted in my seat. "I've told you that it won't make a difference."

He'd been bringing up the medication he wanted me to try for weeks now. One of the main focuses of our sessions was my...intense dreams. He knew in general that they were sexual —the staff had told him that. But he'd never pressed me on specific details—thank god. Dr. Adams seemed to be under the impression I wasn't going to be trapped in this place for the rest of my life if I could get my dreams under control.

He seemed to think that was the main concern and not the fact that I was being held hostage here because of my father.

Dr. Adams leaned forward. "If you could just stay on it for a while, enough to convince them you're ready to be released—"

I squeezed my can so hard that orange soda went everywhere.

"Shit," I gasped, attempting to use my shirt to blot at the soda now all over the leather couch. Frustrated tears built in my eyes as I wiped. I knew what would happen—I would go on those pills but would still be trapped here, of course, and I'd lose even more when I began to walk around in a daze.

Suddenly, his hand was on mine, and I looked to see that he was crouched in front of me. This close to him, it was almost unbearable. He was so fucking beautiful.

"Blake," he murmured, his gaze searching my face. "I'm sorry. You can tell me if there's something else going on."

My lip trembled, and I was very much aware that his fingers were softly caressing my hand. I wanted to tell him about my father, and how I'd ended up here. I wanted to so fucking bad.

I opened my mouth, the story on the tip of my tongue, but then I remembered my father's warning the day I'd been dropped off. I remembered the way the staff had reacted when I'd even dared to say that I wasn't crazy.

Dr. Adams was my only safe space here. I didn't want to ruin that on a pipe dream.

"I'm fine, Dr. Adams. I'm so sorry I've made such a mess," I finally said stiffly, watching as disappointment leached into his features.

"Steele," he said as he pulled his hand away and stood up.

"Steele?" I asked, confused, and hating that I missed his touch.

"You should call me Steele." I watched as he went and grabbed some paper towels from a shelf in the back corner of the room and then walked back over and methodically cleaned up the rest of my spilled drink.

"Oh. Okay." I had to have cracked. That was the only way to explain what was happening. I mean, maybe to a normal girl it wouldn't have seemed like much—the special drink, the hand touch, the first name. But for me, it was a lot. A hell of a lot.

After throwing away the towels, he sat back down in his chair, and he asked his normal questions.

I responded with my usual answers, but everything felt different. I could feel it in the air. I could see it in his eyes. Something had changed.

And as his hand brushed the small of my back as he

opened the door at the end of our session, I wondered what I'd done to make the universe hate me so much.

Because in this life, I could never have Steele or anything else that I wanted. Even if he wanted me.

I walked down the hall away from him, feeling the heat of his stare caressing my back, but I didn't look his way.

The only comfort I was ever going to get in this forsaken place was in my dreams.

With my monsters.

I had to live with that.

Chapter 2
Blake

Three brutal years at Bright Meadows Asylum. And not one visitor.

Until today...

I tried to shake off the weird, ominous feeling that had stretched across my skin ever since one of the staff had come to take me to Dr. Adams' office, where apparently my guests were waiting.

Although Andrew, the asshole, wouldn't tell me who the visitor was, I knew it had to be my parents...which was terrifying. I didn't have anyone else in my life who would have shown up besides them.

I paused in front of Dr. Adams' office door, finding it difficult to make myself knock. I bit my lip as I tried to prepare myself. Was I ready to face them?

You've got this, Blake. Deep breath. And if it is your parents, try not to throw any sharp objects at their heads.

The thought made me smile. If they wanted crazy, I could show them how looney I could get. I'd had a lot of time to perfect that here.

I shook my head and sighed, knowing that would only end

with me in the isolation rooms where the real crazies were kept. Rooms with actual padded walls.

I'd been locked up in one on my arrival...and it had messed with my head for weeks afterward.

Drawing in a trembling breath, I knocked on the door, trying not to let myself get my hopes up that maybe they were here to finally let me out. I could move away, far away, and they'd never have to see or worry about what I'd do again.

"Enter," Dr. Adams answered in that deep voice that captivated me.

I pushed open the door, instantly catching Mother's harsh voice at the doctor before she twisted to look at me with a forced smile. But it vanished as quickly as it came. Her lips pinched with that look of disappointment she'd mastered.

She hadn't seen me for three years, and she could barely hold a smile. I shouldn't have expected anything less.

Ignoring the small pang in my chest, I shut the door and made my way to the empty chair beside her.

"Hi, Mother," I said with a strong tone, refusing to let her see me cower. I wouldn't give her that satisfaction.

"My darling daughter," she responded in a sickly sweet voice that made me want to puke. I saw no evidence of her affection to match her words.

She was a chameleon and knew how to perfectly work a room, to say the right things, even if they were lies. "Blake, you are looking pale." She eyed my gray t-shirt and matching tie-string pants. "And gray isn't your color, dear."

"I'd rather think it brings out my blue eyes," I answered and took my seat, catching the small grin tugging at the corner of Steele's mouth.

He sat across the desk from us in his white button-up shirt done up to his throat today, his bent arms resting on the table, studying us. He was the kind of man that you could get lost for hours just staring at and admiring his features. The kind of hotness that was really good at distracting you from your troubles. The doctor exuded confidence and an aura which had always calmed me. His presence alone made this visitation bearable. He was the one thing that had kept me sane in this insane institute.

On the bright side, there was no sign of Father, which made breathing easier. Perhaps I was about to learn that they'd split up, and somehow in her cold-hearted soul, she'd found enough empathy to help me.

She sat stiffly on the chair, legs crossed. She was wearing her rose-colored wrap-around blazer dress and matching heels, looking completely out of place in the warmly decorated room. Pins kept her hair fixed around her face, dark locks cascading over her shoulders. As always, she looked immaculate. Nothing was ever out of place with her.

Directing her attention to Steele, she asked, "I was promised she would be taken care of. Is she eating enough and getting sufficient sun? The girl looks deathly."

I blinked at her. She talked about me as though she was leaving her pet poodle at the doggie daycare. My hands curled into balls by my side, and I remembered my therapy lessons on anger management about breathing deeply and letting go of emotions.

They weren't doing much to help right then in Mother's company.

I eyed the stapler on the desk and mulled over how good it would feel to throw it at her. I'd picked up a penchant for throwing things since moving in here, which was really my only release and mostly came in the form of destroying my pillow. I was on my fourth one. Steele encouraged me to get my anger out that way, saying it was better done in my room when no one saw.

He obviously didn't know about the camera in there that was always watching me.

"Ma'am, I assure you, Blake receives the utmost care at Bright Meadows Asylum. Now, following procedures, I will remain in the room during your visitation. Normally, we hold these in the main visitors' room, but seeing this is a unique situation, I'll make an exception."

"What situation?" I asked, trepidation sliding up my spine.

Mother sighed, and I watched the transformation of her worried face morphing into something sorrowful, shadows flaring behind her eyes, darkening now. She would have made an amazing actress, able to change her emotions in the blink of an eye. But I suppose the skill worked well for her as a politician's wife.

"Your father has died," she murmured with no difficulty, no tears shed. "I know this will be hard for you, Blake, to lose your dad. Maybe it gives you solace to know that he truly cared for you, wanting only the best care for you by placing you in here."

My chest constricted, and it had nothing to do with my father dying. I didn't give two fucks about that, and I'd often wished that he'd died long ago. But for her to spread blatant lies in front of Steele infuriated me. It burned across my chest, coming at me in waves so hard that a sharp ache rose in my stomach.

Three years of her silence, and now this.

I couldn't hold it back, and my words streamed out. "He never cared for me, Mother. So, let's not pretend by spreading lies."

When you lived in a house of deception and hatred, there was no spark of grief for those who made your life hell. Only relief.

"Don't be so insensitive," she griped. "Your father is barely cold in his grave and you'd dare to speak so harshly of him."

"Wait, you've already buried him? Did you have a funeral?" I hated that I even cared, but it would have given me a chance to get out of here. For at least a little bit.

Mother huffed. "I didn't think it would be good for your mental state to attend, dear."

I reared back in my seat, and instantly, I lost all ability to remember any of my lessons on remaining calm.

"Are you kidding me? The only reason I'm in here is because I caught Father fucking Ryan, Dale, and Stacey...at the same time. There's nothing wrong with me, but if he's dead, he deserves it. And you should know the truth."

Everything came blurting out, words I'd held safely in my head for the past few years but had been dying to say. My father had threatened me from talking about what I witnessed, but with him dead, I wasn't going to hold back anymore.

And I desperately wanted Steele to know the truth.

Mother paused, the color draining from her face, and she eyed me like she'd morphed into the grim reaper coming to collect my soul. "Blake, you are sick, and only a crazy person would make up such horrible stories."

"Ma'am, we don't call anyone sick or crazy here," Steele interjected, sounding calm despite my outburst.

She turned to him with hatred in her eyes. "I do apologize you have to hear the filthy lies she tells. The strain she has put on our family is unbearable."

"Strain?" I stated, balancing on the edge of my chair, interjecting before Steele could say anything.

"Blake," he warned in the darker tone he used to remind me to take a deep breath. To reel my anger back in.

My words rushed out regardless as anger swallowed me. "I've been locked in here for over three fucking years because of his lies."

Without a word, Mother stood, straightened her dress, and collected the rose jacket hanging on the back of her seat. She held her head high, her cheeks flushed from the embarrassment I'd caused her. It was hard to tell if she knew about Father's deceit or if this was a real shock for her.

"You are ill, Blake, and this is the best place to make you better. You may not know it now, but one day, you'll thank your father and me." She glanced at the doctor as she talked, because everything she did was for show.

I bit my tongue until it hurt, until I tasted blood in my mouth and no longer felt the thundering ache tearing across my chest. For so long I'd played the quiet daughter, and I'd let them walk all over me.

"Please do not make a scene," Mother continued. "I've come to let you know the tragic news of your father. Let's leave it at that." She looked ready to leave, and I jolted to my feet, which had Steele doing the same.

"Please, wait."

She turned to me with fury pulling her manicured eyebrows together. Which was a feat considering how much botox I knew she got every couple of months.

"With Father gone, you can dissolve the conservatorship and get me out of here. I've spent long enough here. Please." Freedom teetered on the edge of my mind, so close I could almost taste it, while I internally cursed myself for lashing out at her. My mother was a vengeful person.

I sensed Steele moving in beside me. "Blake, your mother and I had been discussing this earlier."

"And?" I stared from him to her, and her grin was fierce. My mind raced with wild scenarios and excuses they'd give me to steal away my freedom, until I grew breathless.

"I'm moving out of the state, dear, and I just signed the papers today to dissolve my conservatorship over you. So you are free." She smirked. "But unfortunately, you're apparently still suffering from episodes, so your release from the asylum will be determined by the board of doctors once you've healed."

I gaped at her, my head spinning. I couldn't move, but stared at her, drawing in her every word.

Silence hung between us, and tears were running down my cheeks. I had zero control over my life, and I fucking hated it.

"You can't do this," my words choked out, my body trembling uncontrollably. "I don't belong here!"

Steele crossed the room and opened the door to his office for my mother to leave, while I wanted the world to crack open and swallow me. This couldn't be happening.

Panic clawed at my heart, and before I could think straight, I reached for my mother, grabbing her arm, my fingernails digging into her arm out of pure desperation on my part.

She barked a yelp, her eyes widening while she ripped her hand free from me.

"Mom, please!" I looked at her for sympathy, for something other than just her icy stare. I stepped closer to her, and she flinched back. That small reaction stung right through my heart.

Steele was suddenly beside me, his arm looping around mine with his warm touch, holding me tightly against him. "Blake, I need you to calm down for me."

Fury drummed through me as the world tilted around me, swirling too fast.

Mother checked her wrist where I drew blood and wiped it away with the pad of her thumb. Lifting her gaze, she scowled. Glancing at the doctor, she barked, "She needs discipline, and maybe you're not the right person. She just attacked me. I hope you intend to punish her for such a crime or I will take this higher."

I gasped aloud and my gut clenched. I stared at her incredulously, wanting to lash out for all the horrible things she and Father did to me.

"This is an emotional situation, a grieving moment," he explained. "I will ensure this is dealt with."

I glared at my mother, so angry, so desperate that I wanted to throttle her, to force her to treat me as her daughter for a change. But I guessed that was too much to ask for.

She flicked her gaze in my direction. "We all have to live with our own demons, dear. Enjoy yours." Then she strolled out of my life. And I knew that would be the last time I'd ever see her.

That bitch.

I fought against Steele's grip, lunging to go after her, but he tightened his hold on my arm and slammed the door to his room, closing us in there alone. Then he spun me around by my shoulders to face him.

"Let me go," my voice crackled with the first tear rolling down my cheek.

"Blake, you can't attack people here. I can only do so much to protect you," he explained in a low, soothing voice that seemed to almost lull me into a false state of calm. "I don't want them to force me to sedate you while you're handling your grief."

"This is not grief for my monster of a father." I fisted my hands, and I wanted to scream. "This is from years of them mentally and emotionally abusing me. From being thrown in here so I was silenced, and now I'm told I have to stay here because I have stress dreams? How the fuck is that fair?" Tears pooled in my eyes, and they blurred the doctor's face while cold rushed through me with the reality of my fucked up circumstance.

"Nothing's changed," Steele tried to explain. "You're progressing nicely, and we focus on that."

Except he was wrong. "I. Don't. Belong. Here," I cried, shaking. "My mother could have taken me out because she knows why I'm really here. I'm innocent."

Steele reached out for me, but I backed away from him because no one would help. No one cared. At this stage, I was crying hysterically, hugging myself, and suddenly the room spun with me, tilting at an angle, while darkness feathered at the edges of my eyes.

And the last words I heard from Steele were, "I just need you to take your pills to stop the nightmares, and I'll do everything I can to set you free."

"You should take it. You'll feel better," the nurse in her white dress persisted as she handed me a small plastic cup with a blue pill inside over the dispensing counter. "It should help calm you down."

The familiar sense of helplessness filled me as it had done before. They'd never offered me this kind of pill before, mostly under Father's instructions, but Nurse Rose was new here and had been monitoring my sleep. She was sweet, and I saw the pity on her face that morning.

"Will it help me sleep?" I whispered over the counter.

She nodded. "It should."

My fingers tightened around this tiny cup with a shaky hand, staring at this crazy little pill. The temptation to take it sat on the edge of my mind, along with the trepidation of what it would do to me.

What if she was right and I could finally have a good night's sleep?

"Are you done already?" a girl lining up behind me snarled and drove a sharp shoulder into mine, causing me to stumble and almost lose my cup. By some miracle, I managed to fumble it but not drop it.

I turned, furious, only to come face to face with Madison—the girl who liked to cut herself and others if given the chance. She creeped me out, because when you looked into her eyes, there was nothing there. Did she even have a soul?

Somehow, all the crazies in this place were drawn to me.

I stumbled out of her way quickly before she became too interested in me.

I glanced up to the orderly watching me. "I need to see you take the pill before you leave, or I'll administer it myself," he stated harshly, his gaze flickering to the line of girls waiting for their morning doses.

A debilitating panic slithered through me that I'd be trapped in this asylum forever, and maybe the nurse was right about the blue pill taking away the dreams.

Without another thought, I popped it into my mouth and swallowed it with no water.

"Open your mouth," the orderly stated, and I did just that, sticking my tongue out. With his approval, I made my way to the TV room.

I don't remember how long I sat on the couch, and I didn't know what I watched—I slouched in my seat lifelessly. It was a strange thing to not feel your body while your mind floated. Escaping my memories was almost liberating though, and I just hoped this sensation helped me sleep peacefully tonight.

Maybe being completely numb wasn't so bad...

A spark of something sharp stuck into my arm. Something I didn't understand right away. I craned my head down to my arm where the girl who'd shoved me out of the line earlier was gripping my arm, her fingernails in my skin, pushing down.

"Ouch," I managed, moments after it happened because my mouth didn't want to move. I had been partially aware of the pain, while thoughts flickered in and out of my mind. But moving to get away from her seemed an impossible thing to do.

"Don't ever push in front of me again, bitch. Next time, I'll cut you until you bleed to death," she snarled in my ear, raking her nails down my arms, breaking the skin.

I cried out that time, and she jolted out of the seat before rushing away. I sat there a second later, staring at the droplets of blood rolling down my arm. And a tinge of worry crawled through me at how vulnerable I felt right now. How I seemed to have forgotten how to even get up from this couch.

I shut my eyes and cradled my cut arm against my middle in my drug-filled haze. And I kept feeling like there was something important I should be doing...

Chapter 3

Blake

The lights were off, and the storm outside darkened the art room. Rain struck on the windowpane, while thunder growled overhead in a musical tune I normally enjoyed.

Today, it got on my nerves, the sound growing repetitive and annoying. It had been one week since my mother's visit, and not even the weather could soothe my mood.

It was the first day I hadn't cried.

This morning, Steele insisted it was a sign of my improvement. In truth, I'd run out of tears. Because on the inside, I still felt as broken and destroyed as the moment Mother sealed my fate in this place.

If you take the pill, you will recover quicker, Blake. The dreams will fade, and you'll have a case to prove you are improving enough to leave.

Bless Steele. He truly did care for me. And as much as I fell victim to his charm and burned all over when he stepped too close to me, when I inhaled his woodsy cologne, when I imagined what it would feel like to have his hands on me, I also couldn't forget how the blue pill made me feel. Numb and useless. It left me vulnerable in a place filled with real crazies who snapped at the drop of a hat.

And the trouble wouldn't end there. Bright Meadows had systems in place where they made sure you stayed on medication after you got out of here as well.

My gaze darted towards Madison. She sat across the room from me now in our team circle of twelve people. Her earlier smile morphed into a threatening scowl at my entrance.

The girl loathed me, and my breath hitched all the way down to my lungs whenever she came near me. For some reason, she hated me from my first encounter with her three years ago. Like several other inmates–I mean patients. Since then, she'd been in my face any chance she got.

Dr. Jamison better hurry up. I glanced back at the open door, willing her to just appear.

Crack.

Several of the patients in class flinched and yelped at the crack of lightning.

I flopped down in a chair next to Ed, the guy who enjoyed smearing his food over his face. He was harmless and left me alone. I liked that.

Madison sat across from me.

Everyone in the circle had fallen silent.

She mumbled something under her breath, at one stage snapping loudly, "You think I don't know that?"

Her shoulders were hunched up, and she appeared terrifying. I once heard the nurses mention Madison having dissociative identity disorder. She apparently suffered from alternate personalities and heard voices talking to her. As a result, she was on heavy medication to help her. Though with the unhinged look in her eyes, I was doubting she took her meds today.

Like with any vicious dog staring you down, I didn't look directly at her and internally wished the therapist would get here already. It really wasn't like her to not be here before us.

Madison got to her feet, gripping something in her closed fist, her dead eyes on me. The only reason I knew that was because someone gasped out loud and I jerked my head up.

Her friend, the only girl mad enough to spend time with Madison, grabbed her shirt. "Mads, sit down. You'll get us all in trouble."

"Block the door, Jen!" she ordered in response.

"Mads," she whined, her face blanching.

"Do it fucking now!"

Jen's shoulders curled forward, but she darted to the door regardless, carrying her chair and jamming the back under the handle.

My heart somersaulted and I jumped to my feet, moving to stand behind my chair, gripping it because every hair on my body stood on end. Of course she was coming for me. She did whenever she got the chance, but something was different about her today.

I wondered which personality I'd encounter... her serial killer one, I bet.

Because she looked genuinely ready to murder me.

With Dr. Jamison not in the room, there'd be no one to stop this crazy bitch from killing me.

"Madison, don't do anything stupid," I said.

"You calling me stupid?" she barked, her lips peeling back over a row of yellow stained teeth.

"N-no. If you do anything, you'll end up in isolation for a very long time." I talked fast when I was nervous, my hands gripping the chair, my knuckles going white.

A girl nearby started crying, while another rushed into the corner and hid behind the curtains.

The others watched with huge eyes, ready to be entertained. Nothing exciting happened in the asylum, so when two patients got into a fight, everyone cheered. No one would help me... because they were too scared of Madison. Too scared of ending up in isolation.

Madison's eyes twitched again, and she looked possessed, as if her face wasn't her own.

"You're in my seat," she barked at me.

"It's yours. Take it," I answered.

She just nodded and smirked as she snatched the chair from my grip and kicked it aside.

Okay, maybe that wasn't such a bright idea to give away my only barricade from crazy eyes here.

"Madison, please," I began, but I never got to finish my sentence. The bitch lashed out with her fist at my face.

I reared back, but not quick enough. A sharp sting sliced across my cheek and halfway across my nose.

I cried out, back peddling, and reached for my face. My fingers come back bloody from where she cut me. It stung like crazy.

A glint of something drew my attention to the razor blade pinched between her fingers.

Was she fucking kidding me? She could have killed me with that one blow. Blinded me.

Terror gripped me, while everyone else in the room was booming with explosive cheers.

But there was no pause. Madison charged me once more, moving too fast. With no weapon for me, because all painting items were kept under lock and key until the therapist arrived, I went old school.

I retaliated with a fist, cracking her square in the nose. A dull, throbbing pain shot up my arm, hurting badly, but seeing Madison groan and stumble backward was the break I needed. Blood splashed from her nose, and I ran for the door.

Jen was there, and I growled, "Get the fuck out of my way."

Something heavy crashed into the back of my legs, and I screamed as my knees buckled out from under me. I fell forward and hit the tiled floor with a loud slap.

I jerked to get up, when Madison landed on my back, straddling me, fisting my hair and wrenching my head back. "Eyes or throat," she snarled. "Which should I cut out first?"

The sickening sound of her sucking in a wet breath had me drawing in my own fast breath. The scrawny bitch was strong, and I didn't dare move when she placed the razor blade in front of my face.

Someone was banging on the door to the room, shouting to open it up. But I couldn't hear anything beyond that and the thumping of my pulse in my ears.

I stared at my reflection in the metal razor, at how terrified and pale I looked. At the blood covering my cheek. At the haunted look reflected in my eyes. The longer I stayed in the asylum, the quicker I'd end up like the rest of them.

Wild.

Lost.

Psychotic.

I held that stare for the longest second, until it burned into my mind of what coming face to face with death looked like.

Echoes of everyone screaming reverberated in the room, and I shook terribly.

"Come on, bitch, or do you want me to choose?" Madison suddenly sliced my other cheek, and I cried out. "I'm all about symmetry. I need to make sure it matches, which means both eyes are coming out."

Perspiration ran down my back, and as she came closer to my eyes, I knew I needed to fight back or I'd end up blind.

Hands flat and toes pressed into the floor, I bucked her off me with every inch of strength I possessed.

She flew off me, screaming.

In that exact same moment, the door shattered open, smashing into several pieces. Everyone screamed madly just as the chair holding the door in place flew directly for me.

I threw myself back to the ground, my cheek flat to the cold tiles as the chair zipped right over me. It scraped down my back and tumbled away.

Booming voices surrounded me, and my heart thundered against my rib cage, trying to break free and escape. I didn't move right away, stunned by what just happened. My fingers dug into the tiles, fighting the panic that flooded me.

"I'm not dead. Not dead. Not dead," I mumble to myself.

Someone suddenly tucked their arms under my armpits, and a flash of terror cut through me.

I flinched and scrambled away from them. "Don't touch me," I shrieked.

Pain flared across my ravaged cheeks, my heart banging in my chest.

Steele was crouching in front of me, worry twisting his gorgeous features. "You're safe now, Blake." He reached out for me. "Can I take you to the infirmary? You're cut up badly."

I'm not dead.

I swallowed hard and fought the scream wedged in my chest that wanted to come out. Other orderlies and therapists burst into the room, three of them needed to wrangle Madison who was slashing her own arms now.

I was trembling hard, and fragments of her attack stuck to my mind on replay. Other patients bellowed out, and some ran from the room.

Chaos. It followed me everywhere.

"Blake," Steele said, bringing me back to him with his hand stroking mine. His touch was soothing, distracting.

I softly leaned toward him. "Please take me away from here."

"I've got you," he said softly, and butterflies burst in my stomach at the tenderness behind his voice, at the heartfelt expression on his face. There was something deep about his eyes today, like a wild animal. Something stirred behind them with fury. He was angry for me, wasn't he?

He lifted me into his arms, and I curled myself against his chest. Steele was a strong man; I could feel his muscles shifting against me. Compared to him, I was tiny.

My muscles quivered, my hands trembled, and I tucked my head against his neck, taking in a deep breath of his cologne. It infiltrated every inch of me, desire shooting through me despite the dire circumstances I'd found myself in.

Dozens of times I'd dreamt of him whisking me out of here...my knight in shining armor rescuing me. I licked my lips and stared up at this man who'd been my rock the last three years.

"You're safe now," he reminded me, rubbing my back.

He carried me out of the art room, and I glanced back at Madison being forced into a straitjacket. She'd be in isolation for a long time after that episode. It didn't soften the terror in my chest at the vivid reminder that I wasn't safe in the asylum.

She hollered, screaming my name with anger.

Next time, she'd kill me. I heard it in her voice, and I winced, curling tighter in Steele's arms.

Thoughts swished through my head, from my father's death, to Mother abandoning me, and to Madison now attempting to murder me.

Memories that would forever haunt me.

For too long, I'd permitted others to walk over me. I'd lived with fear.

I didn't want to end up staying in this asylum any longer than I needed to, and considering my choices had dried out, I made a decision to fight for my freedom. Even if it made me feel sick and numbed me, nothing was worse than sleeping under the same roof as a killer who was out for my blood.

"I want to take the pills," I whispered in Steele's ear. "Please help me end my nightmares."

Chapter 4

Blake

Two Months Later

The rain sliced across my skin as I hurried down the block towards my apartment. I kept throwing glances behind me continually just in case someone tried to sneak up behind me.

Life after the asylum...had been difficult. Considering my time at Bright Meadows had robbed me of a high school diploma, and everything else, and I had no family or friends I could rely on—I didn't have very many options.

Bright Meadows had a program sponsored by the state to help its "residents" assimilate back into society.

That "program" meant putting me in a crappy apartment in the worst part of town. Drug deals happened in the hallway right outside my room and gunshots sounded outside constantly as the city gangs fought over territory. I'd had a bullet come through the thin wall just last week right as I'd come home from work, and I'd almost had a heart attack.

Needless to say, the place wasn't great.

The only job I'd been able to find was at the city library

ten blocks away, working the graveyard shift. The library was open twenty-four hours for some reason, but the only patrons that filled the book stacks at night were the homeless. I spent my hours putting away books and cleaning since the city had decided the library staff should be the one doing the cleaning instead of a janitorial crew.

Picking up used needles in the bathroom stalls wasn't ideal, but I got to read a lot, which was something I never got to do at Bright Meadows. And I was just lucky that Ms. Juniper, the crusty head librarian who looked around a hundred years old, had taken a chance on me.

As grateful as I was for the job, working the graveyard shift hours was a bit terrifying when it meant I had to walk home at four am in the roughest part of town, and then would lose the rest of the day thanks to the medicine I was still forced to take.

In a perfect world, I would have stopped the medicine the second I got out, but I'd always known that wouldn't be a possibility. To ensure that I remained on the pills, the state had actually instituted that I take weekly drug tests that monitored the levels of the medicine in my system. I had to take the pill as soon as I got home, and then I would lose the whole day to my brain fog. It would wear off slightly starting around two hours before my shift, but I was still drowsy and forced to work with a head that felt like it was full of cotton throughout the night. I'd hoped that over time my body would get used to the medicine, but so far, I'd had the same terrible reaction every single day.

Although most people would have described my life as miserable, it felt better to be out of Bright Meadows than in it.

I made it to my apartment complex, pushing on the worthless gate that was supposed to protect the residents but hadn't had a functioning lock since I'd moved in. I walked up the steps, exhausted and feeling like I was going to collapse, and then almost burst into tears when I saw that the door to my apartment was wide open.

Just what I was looking forward to today–my first break-in.

My heart hammered in my chest as I stood there. I could tell that whoever had done it wasn't there anymore since I was able to see every inch of the place from the doorway. My apartment consisted of one room. The sofa against the wall across from me, with its worn-out springs, served as my bed and the chipped coffee table in front of it served as my dining table. I was relieved to see they were both still there despite the fact that most people would have thrown them away years ago. There was a toilet and a small shower in the left corner of the room, but there wasn't a wall or privacy curtain around either. My stomach twisted when I saw that the door to the fridge and freezer had been left wide open, showcasing the now empty interior. I'd just stopped for groceries the day before, and I wasn't due to be paid for another week. Anything I had left from my last paycheck had to cover my electricity bill.

I guess I would be living without electricity for a bit since it seemed a bit daunting thinking of trying to survive a week without eating anything.

I walked over to close the doors to the refrigerator and flinched when I realized how cold the freezer was. This meant that the break-in had literally just happened because the ice hadn't defrosted at all yet and the fridge was still cold as well. My room was too hot even on its best day, so things would have melted by now if it had been a bit since someone had been in here.

What if I had been here? What if I'd taken my pill already and I'd just been lying on the couch, completely lost to my surroundings?

I trembled and bit my lip as I continued to struggle not to burst into tears.

That was it. I wasn't going to take another one of those pills. I had a drug test two days from now, and they would know what I'd done, but I was just going to have to figure it out. I wasn't going back to Bright Meadows, and even though they would definitely kick me out of my apartment and try to force me back in there, I was never going to take one of those pills again.

I immediately felt at peace with my decision, and I even found myself whistling as I pushed the coffee table against the door and hooked the security chain to the wall so I'd at least have some warning if someone tried to break in again. I grabbed the rockstar romance I'd borrowed from the library and settled into the couch, trying to ignore my racing thoughts. Eventually, even with how violated I felt about someone being in my space, and my uncertainty over my future, I drifted off to a deep, dreamless sleep.

...

I'd forgotten what it felt like to have energy. But even skipping one dose of the medicine had me feeling like a new person as I hustled around the library completing the list of tasks that Ms. Juniper had given me. The library doors chimed, signaling that someone was coming in, and I automatically looked over, only to almost drop the stack of books I was carrying when I saw who it was.

It was Steele. Intense longing erupted through me as we locked eyes. He looked so fucking good. Unlike the stiff businessman outfit he rocked at Bright Meadows, he was dressed in a worn pair of jeans and a tight black shirt that showcased every single muscle in his body. There was a couple of drunk prostitutes flipping through magazines at a table nearby, and they were greedily eyeing him like fresh meat.

I'd seen Steele bi-weekly for state-mandated appointments,

and we'd discussed where I worked, but I hadn't expected him to come here. My stomach clenched as my mind came up with the worst-case possibilities. He was here to tell me that I had to return to Bright Meadows. The state somehow knew already that I'd stopped taking my meds. I had a long list of possible bad things that could have happened.

I went back to my task of organizing returned books on my cart, very much aware of his gaze on my back, but determined to delay any bad news for as long as he would let me. When I'd finished that task, I walked over to the librarian's desk and pretended to look busy.

Because I was obviously awkward like that.

Steele wandered towards my desk with a small smile on his lips that I really wanted to kiss away. He leaned over the counter, tapping his fingers lightly on the wood, and I found myself thinking what sexy hands he had. Was that a thing? Because if it was a thing, Steele would win all the awards.

I finally looked up at him, and my breath caught as his gaze danced all over my face, so much yearning in the icy blue depths of his eyes that I suddenly felt hot all over.

"What are you doing here?" I asked, pretending to be scribbling on a notepad just in case Ms. Juniper decided to poke her head out of her office and yell at me.

"We haven't got much time to talk lately. I missed you," he responded in a silky, panty-melting voice.

I lost the ability to speak with that answer. Ever since I'd gotten out of Bright Meadows, he'd been polite, but he hadn't made any more comments that told me he was interested.

I'd begun to think I'd imagined it all.

"Has something changed that I should know about?" I asked softly. His hand reached out and took one of my hands, his thumb sliding against my skin in a way that sent shivers slipping down my spine.

"I couldn't wait anymore," he said softly. "I thought I'd

give you time to get settled before letting you know how I feel, but it's killing me not to touch you, to be able to talk to you every day, to be there for you."

For a second I absorbed his lovely words, and the warmth of his touch, the first I'd had from someone since the last time he touched my hand after I made a fool of myself by spilling soda everywhere.

"I have to get back to work," I told him, gently pulling my hand away.

"I'm not going anywhere, baby," he murmured, and I stiffened, my mouth dropping open in disbelief. He shrugged sheepishly. "I've been calling you that in my head for a long time."

I closed my mouth and scurried away like a scared mouse, picking up books left on tables and throwing trash away that I found on the floor. I must have been working at twice my normal speed compared to when I was coming off my meds, because sooner than I would have liked with Steele still here, I couldn't think of anything else to do.

I finally walked back to where he was seated at a table and sat down across from him.

"You're angry at me," he said, no question in his voice.

I thought about that for a moment. I didn't know what I was. I wasn't angry so much as it felt like this was something that couldn't go anywhere. Even if I was desperate for it.

Because he was the doctor who prescribed my medications, and now that I'd already decided I was never going to take that stuff again, it seemed a bit like a major conflict of interest.

I rubbed my temples with both hands, a headache forming right behind my eyes.

"I thought maybe you were interested in me as well," he asked tentatively, his face the most vulnerable that I'd ever seen it.

I bit my lip and studied the small crack in the table in front of me as I thought about what I should say.

"You know that I am," I finally answered softly, unable to lie about the fact that I'd been crazy about him since the moment I'd seen him.

"Blake," a low voice called out from behind me.

I turned around and almost fell out of the chair when I saw who was calling me. The man standing at the entrance of the dining hall was a god, that was the only way to explain how gorgeous he was. I'd never come close to seeing someone as good-looking as him in my entire life.

His eyes widened when he saw me, and I tried to nonchalantly wipe my face, just in case some food was hanging out on my chin.

"Are you ready for our session?"

Session. Right. My insides shrunk when I realized that he must be the psychiatrist that everyone was always talking about. And now I understood why.

I got out of my chair and walked towards him, trying not to look too eager. He was probably as sadistic as everyone else was here. As I got within reach of him, he held out his hand for me to shake. I jumped when our fingers grazed, an electric shock propelling through my body.

"I'm Steele Adams," he'd murmured, his otherworldly gaze staring at me so intensely that I was sure he could see right into my soul.

Ms. Juniper called my name just then, and I was yanked from my trip down memory lane. I jumped out of my seat and darted towards her. She had fired two employees just last week when she thought they were flirting with patrons instead of working, and I didn't want to be her next casualty.

I knew better than to sit near library patrons. Steele had evidently caused me to lose my head for a moment.

Her lips were pursed tightly in disapproval as I got to

where she was standing. "The place is dead. I'll have Elizabeth cover the next hour and you can go home," she snapped, turning around to head back into her office.

"But I can still come for my shift tomorrow?" I asked, trying to feel her mood out, and she nodded, looking at me strangely.

"Okay, thanks," I murmured, knowing she wouldn't care even if I did try and explain how much it affected me losing even one hour of my paycheck.

Steele was standing when I turned around.

"Be right back," I mouthed, and he nodded as I strode towards the back room where my meager belongings were stored.

Steele was still there when I came out, even though I'd been deliberately slow.

"Can I buy you a cup of coffee?" he asked, sounding nervous. I nodded hesitantly. I wasn't sure what I wanted from him at the moment.

We walked together towards the exit, his hand brushing against my lower back as he held the door to the outside open and ushered me through the doors.

It had stopped raining after the last three days full of storms, and the air smelled fresh and clean for the time being as we strode out into the darkness.

We walked out to the sidewalk and Steele stopped in his tracks, a sound of dismay slipping from his beautiful lips.

"What's wrong?" I asked.

"I'm actually not sure what's open at this time of night," he answered with a frown.

"There's a diner two blocks down," I offered. "It's relatively non-sketchy."

"Perfect," he said, grabbing my hand as we began to walk.

I stared at our interlocked hands in fascination, my heart

racing as I almost tripped on a crack in the sidewalk. What if I could have him like this every day?

No sooner had that thought crossed my mind, all the reasons why I couldn't ever be with him had me stopping in my tracks.

"I don't think this is a good idea," I said softly, feeling defeated as the words slipped from my mouth.

He looked adorably confused. "I think it's the best idea ever. In fact, I've only been thinking about this idea since the moment I met you."

"You do remember you met me in an insane asylum, right?" I drawled. "And I'm pretty sure it's against the rules of ethics for you to date your own patient. I know I read that somewhere."

"I don't care about that sort of thing," he commented.

"Then you regularly date your patients?" I asked cooly.

He flushed. "No, never. But the alternative is that I resign as your doctor and the state makes you see Dr. Riggins, and I'm not going to let that happen."

"I'm not going to be taking those pills anymore," I blurted out.

He looked panicked at my statement. "Blake, you have to take them. It's incredibly important, especially now that you're out —" he began.

I yanked my hand away from his and took a step back.

"Are you going to report me?" I snapped, betrayal slicing through my heart.

Steele looked shocked by my question. "What? Of course not, but they're still testing you..."

"I don't care. I'm going to figure something out. But I can't do it anymore. This isn't living," I said calmly.

Steele's panic increased and he took a step towards me, holding up his hands beseechingly. "Blake," he began. "Even if you weren't still being monitored, you have to stop those dreams. You can't let them in." He closed his eyes and cursed.

"Let who in?" I asked, very confused.

"Just listen to me, please. Keep taking your pills."

I shook my head and began to back further away. "I've already lost years of my life, Steele. I'm not going to lose anymore," I said softly before turning and walking away. He didn't follow me, and obviously, that was for the best.

But it didn't stop the tears from flowing down my face the entire walk home. I hadn't realized how much I'd let him in until now.

I wondered if there was ever going to be anyone in this world for me, or if I was going to be doomed to be alone forever.

...

When I got home, my apartment door was blissfully closed and I sighed in relief as I unlocked it and looked around my little hovel. Home sweet home.

After washing my face, I curled up on the couch, my mind racing with all the things I had to figure out. But eventually, all the crying and being up all night working caught up to me, and I fell into a deep sleep.

And when I did, for the first time in months, he was waiting for me...

My monster.

He'd spread my legs, and he was staring down at me with a dark, possessive look.

"I've been waiting for you, Pet. Have you missed me?" he asked as he softly circled my clit with the sharp tip of his claw.

"Yes," I moaned. "You disappeared. I've been all alone."

"I've thought about nothing but eating this sweet pussy. You're never going to be alone again." He shoved my legs open

even wider, and a second later his mouth was on my pulsing clit, licking and sucking on it and making sounds so erotic that I was close to coming within seconds. He suckled my clit for a few minutes more before beginning to fuck my slit with his mouth, his tongue thrusting in and out of me, and I knew I was gushing all over his face.

"You taste so fucking good, my sweet," he growled as his wet tongue slid between my folds, circling my clit again, and then plunging back into my opening so that he was consuming every drop of my arousal. I was moaning embarrassingly loud, but I couldn't take my eyes off of him between my legs. My insides began to clench as my orgasm approached and then...

"Yes," I cried out, just as my eyes flew open.

Only to realize that I was wide awake and there was still someone between my legs devouring and licking all over my clenching pussy.

Chapter 5

Blake

I screamed when I saw the long black horns sticking up from his head, and the monster from my dreams looked up at the sound and gave me a sharp-toothed smile. "Hello, Pet," he said, amused, his forked tongue darting out to lick off the arousal that was coating his lips.

I screamed even louder and tried to pull away, but his claws were wrapped around my legs, keeping them pushed apart. Before I could blink, he sat up and shoved his thighs between my legs before spearing me with his two-headed cock that I was very familiar with from my dreams.

I came instantly, my back arching as my moans filled the small room. His abs flexed as he began to move in and out of me.

"Good girl," he groaned as he thrust into me brutally with his long length. A rush of pleasure flowed over me and I forgot all about the fact that a literal monster was fucking me right now. I had to still be asleep; that was the only way that I could rationalize this. And since I had to be sleeping, I might as well enjoy the best sex I could imagine.

"You're perfect for us," he murmured, before groaning. "Fuck, you're squeezing my dick so tight. You love this, Pet. You can't get enough of it, can you?"

When I didn't answer him because I was about to orgasm again, he grabbed my chin and forced me to look at him, the tips of his claws digging softly into my skin.

His red eyes were glowing intensely as he stared at me, and I couldn't look away. "Answer me," he ordered as he began to pound into me with an even more brutal pace.

"Yes, yes, yes! I love it," I cried as my whole body clenched and I fell off the cliff into the most devastating orgasm he'd given me yet.

My monster came with a loud roar that shook the glass in the windows, and then he collapsed on top of me.

It took a full minute for my brain to start working again, and for me to realize that there was literally a monster from my dreams, with horns and claws, sharp teeth and a forked tongue, on top of me right now.

I began to thrash underneath him, desperately trying to get him off of me despite the fact that he probably outweighed me by several hundred pounds. His claws raked through my hair softly as if I was being completely still, not seeming bothered at all by my attempts to get away.

"It doesn't need to be like this, my sweet," he said with a benign smile like I really was an adorable little pet he was amusedly watching. His dick was still inside of me, and when he lifted his head, it rocked against my walls, scattering sensations throughout my whole body that had me ready for more.

I blinked, and all of a sudden, an incredibly gorgeous man had replaced the one with monstrous features—a human man.

"Is this better?" he purred as he continued to stroke my hair, and everything went black as I passed out from pure shock.

...

I woke up to the most delicious smell I'd ever experienced. I opened my eyes blearily, still exhausted.

I froze as the fridge door opened. Everything that had happened flashed through my brain, and I had to force myself to look over to the tiny kitchen area where, sure enough, the blonde Adonis who had appeared between my legs was concentrating hard on something he was stirring on my tiny camp stove while also pulling food out of the refrigerator with his other hand. He had definitely not been there when I went to sleep.

He was wearing a frilly apron that had a huge heart on it that said "Kiss the cook."

It was official—I'd lost my mind.

I really wished I could blame this whole experience on getting drunk or high in a cool dive bar and bringing home a hot stranger, but obviously, that was not the case.

I sat further up and he turned around, flashing me a gorgeous smile, his teeth white and even, no sign of the fangs I was very familiar with.

"Don't try and convince yourself otherwise, my pet," he said in a lilting, familiar voice that I'd heard for years. "I am what you humans call a monster, and I was just in between your legs."

I pinched my arm and he raised an amused eyebrow.

"Not going to work, sweetheart. Pancakes?" he asked, lifting up his skillet.

"Pancakes?" I repeated stupidly.

"Yes. That's one of your favorite foods, isn't it?" He grabbed a plate I definitely hadn't had before and then slid three perfectly fluffy pancakes onto it before grabbing a bottle of pure maple syrup—that I also hadn't had—and pouring it on top of the pancakes with a flourish.

"Fuck, I should've asked if you like butter on top of your flapjacks," he muttered, glaring at the stack of carbs like they'd personally offended him.

"It's official. I've lost my mind," I garbled as I flung myself off the couch, wondering how I was going to get myself out of this dream.

Although, the pancakes really did smell good. Maybe it wouldn't hurt to have a bite before exiting this weird-ass hallucination.

He walked over to me and set the pancakes down on the coffee table before gently lifting my chin to look up at him. "Eat, Pet," he growled softly, his golden eyes staring into mine. They were the exact shade of gold as the flecks of gold scattered throughout his red monster eyes. I got lost in them for a second before he gently pushed me down onto the couch. When I still didn't make a move to touch the pancakes, he sat on the coffee table next to the plate and speared a bite onto a fork before lifting it up to my lips. I opened my mouth automatically and then groaned as the taste of the pancakes hit my tongue.

"These are fucking amazing," I gasped as I chewed, automatically opening up my mouth for more as a low purr reverberated through his chest. I anxiously looked at him only to be shocked with how pleased he looked at the fact that I was enjoying what he'd made.

"Your cupboards were a little bare, Blake," he murmured as I took another bite. "It's a good thing you've finally let me back in. I can make sure you're always taken care of now."

"Let you back in?" I asked, trying to ignore the warmth his promise to take care of me had created in my chest. His gaze turned almost feral when I licked off a drop of syrup on my bottom lip.

"Those pills you've been taking have been blocking us

from getting to you, Pet," he explained, as he tried to feed me another bite.

I shook my head, scooting as far back into the couch as I could to get some space from his overwhelming presence.

"I'm sorry. This is a lot. Obviously," I said, biting my lip and trying to ignore the way he was looking at me, because it was so overwhelming. His gaze was worshipful, possessive... crazy. And obviously, something was very, very wrong with me because I loved it.

I flushed as everything sunk in. "This is real. And if this is real, then..."

"We've been fucking regularly for the last few years?" he finished for me. "I own every inch of your delectable body?" he growled.

My panties were immediately soaked as a million nights of dreams where he'd fucked me everywhere flashed through my mind. He and the others.

"The others are real too," I gasped, looking around the room like they were going to pop out at any minute. Why was I being so calm about all of this? My heart was pounding, but the urge to run I should have been feeling was non-existent. Even in this unfamiliar form, he felt important to me, like his essence had wrapped around something inside of me. Every cell in my body was telling me not to be afraid of him.

"The others are going crazy not being able to see you. Perks of being king, I suppose, that I get to be the one to bring you home."

Home. The word reverberated through me, and I leaned forward as if he'd spoken a magic password.

"You like that, don't you? You know you belong with me...belong with us," he murmured in a low, throaty voice that shot lust through my veins.

I shook my head, trying to undo the spell his voice and his

words had spun. "Can I see you again?" I asked, and he smiled wickedly.

"Your wish is my command," he hummed. I blinked and there he was again, the monster that was more familiar to me at this point in my life than anything or anyone else. My gaze ran over his familiar features, and I wondered what was wrong with me that something inside of me liked this form...more.

"My dreams were real," I whispered again as I reached out and tentatively touched his face, feeling beyond shy even though just a bit ago I'd been holding onto those delicious horns for dear life as he fucked me into the couch.

His eyes closed and he shivered as my fingers brushed against his smooth skin. When he opened his eyes again, his pupils were blown out so much that the red and gold was almost completely hidden.

"Creed," he said suddenly.

"Creed?" I repeated.

"That's my name."

"Creed," I said again, and he once again shivered.

"Fuck. I love that," he growled as his forked tongue briefly flicked out from his mouth.

A gunshot just outside my window shattered the moment like broken glass, and I quickly jerked my hand back, ignoring the disappointment on his face at the loss of my touch.

Creed reached towards the plate and got another bite of pancakes, but this time he didn't use a fork. "I need you to finish this before we leave. You've lost far too much weight."

A small shiver flashed down my spine at the command in his voice, and I found myself opening my mouth to obey him, unable to refuse. My lips closed carefully over his fingers as I took the bite and licked the syrup from his offered claws.

When his words finally sunk in, I jerked away. "Where exactly are you trying to take me...and why?"

"Trying to take you?" he commented amusedly, shaking his head. "My people need to feed," he said gently, softly stroking a clawed finger down my cheek, sending the butterflies in my stomach into flight.

"Feed?" I gasped, really not liking the sound of that. My eyes were immediately drawn to the two sharp fangs sticking out from his mouth.

"Are you some kind of vampire? Is this where you and the others bleed me dry?"

He laughed, and the sound rolled over my skin. Nope, I was not going to think about how much I liked hearing it.

"I'm much better than any bloodsucker," he commented.

Right. Obviously, vampires were real as well.

"For the last five hundred or so years, my people have fed off fear. Every nightmare, every scream, every child's fear as they laid in the dark...we could absorb in our realm, the fear feeding our powers. And for a long time, that was enough."

His gaze tripped over my lips, and his forked tongue peeked out again before he dragged his eyes back to mine.

"And then society changed. Humans began to be desensitized by all the violence, and the horror films, and the twenty-four-hour news coverage that got them accustomed to chaos. The fear began to dry up and we had to find other ways to survive. It took some trial and error, but eventually, we realized we could feed off lust. And that was something in complete abundance in this realm."

He chuckled darkly, the gold in his red eyes brightening until his eyes looked like they were glowing.

"The only problem was, unlike with fear, which could last us for a few weeks, lust only lasted a few hours. My circle and I were forced to feed constantly in order to give my people enough power."

I stared at him with wide eyes, trying to imagine monsters feeding, and then a thought struck me. They'd obviously been feeding off of my lust by—"So you just went around fucking everyone in their dreams?" I asked, wincing when I realized how jealous I sounded and quickly looked away.

He chuckled lowly and used the tip of his long black claw to tip my gaze up to his as he seemed to like to do. "It wasn't quite like that, Pet. We would go from dream to dream, just hovering there, soaking in the men and women's erotic dreams as they fantasized about everything they could do if they weren't trapped in their boring lives. It worked, but it had us spending far too long away from the realm, which wasn't safe for my people."

I jumped when something wrapped around my hair, and I glanced in alarm to the side to see that his tail had wrapped itself around my hair like a fist.

"And then I discovered you," he purred as his tongue darted out and licked at my lips. I trembled and he grinned wickedly. "You were having a dream about that doctor of yours," he growled, and this time, he was the one who sounded jealous. The butterflies in my stomach were swarming now as the hot length of his tail let my hair go and began to softly drag its tip down my spine. "I found myself visiting night after night so I could watch you, and then one night—I'm not sure what came over me, but I decided to take over the dream like I'd been craving. And when I did that, I realized that the energy from that could feed my people for months…"

"But I had dreams with you and the others every night…" I said slowly, yelping when the tail suddenly smacked the top of my ass. Creed's claw softly dragged down my side, and then he gently rubbed where his tail had just set my skin on fire.

"The energy came with strings, Pet. Strings that I didn't mind. Although it didn't seem to affect my people at all, my circle and I became…addicted. I probably could have gone much longer without your sweet little body—but I'm a king, and kings are generally known for their indulgence."

My cheeks flushed as his tail dragged back up my spine, and my mind got caught on a particularly crazy dream where Creed had been fucking me in my pussy...while his tail had taken my ass.

"But why didn't you try other humans to see if it was the same?" I asked, detesting how much I hated the thought of them touching anyone but me.

"Tempest tried a bunch of others, and the energy level from anyone else but you lasted just a few hours as well. You're special, Pet."

"Tempest," I mused, trying to picture which monster would be named that. My mind immediately went to one that would stay in the shadows, only taking me from behind so I wouldn't see his face. He'd always had a dark energy that almost seemed to slither down my skin. I wondered if that was his name.

I glanced back over Creed's features with a frown as I thought of something. "It's been months. You don't seem any worse for the wear," I commented, blushing inanely as the words came out because it made me think of just how...attractive I found him in this form.

His gaze darkened and a flicker of fear sparked across my skin. "That's only because I've just fucked you for hours and gotten my fill. The last few months have been...hell. I'll never allow you to be away from me like that again." Creed glanced over to where the pills were laying at the end of the couch where I'd tossed them once I'd decided not to take them anymore. He grabbed the bottle and squeezed, and I gasped, shocked, as the bottle and the pills dissolved into nothing but a fine powder. "I couldn't come to this realm without you having a dream that would allow me through. I've spent every second waiting for you."

Something warm unfurled in my chest. He'd waited for me.

What about Steele? a voice reminded me, and his handsome face filled my head. That image served as a cold bucket of water to the fantasy world my monster was creating.

My monster. It should have felt crazy to think those words, but after three years of being so intimate with someone...every single night...there was no way to describe it.

"You want to take me with you to feed on me," I said quietly. "How will that be any better than my life here?"

Creed used his tail to push me closer to him.

"Well, I'm sure the orgasms would be an improvement," he purred.

I frowned. "That's what you're offering me?"

"I've found that orgasms do lead to happiness."

I scoffed. "I'm good, thank you. I don't think that what you're offering me sounds like something I'm interested in."

Something in Creed's chest rumbled.

"I'm afraid, Pet, that it's not an option for you to be anywhere but with me," he declared, pulling me even closer.

Right as I tried to move out of his arms, his tail whipped the air behind me. I blinked...and the room around us disappeared. I briefly glimpsed a world of gray spirals that melted into an inky black sky, and then the world slipped away as I lost consciousness.

Ash

"Stop fidgeting," my twin barked gruffly as I paced back and forth.

"I can't help it. I can feel her," I moaned like a fucking brat. "Creed's just trying to torture us at this point. We've been desperate for her too."

Seven growled in response, and I rolled my eyes at the

sound. He was just as anxious for Blake to be here as I was. It had been months since I'd tasted her, since I'd felt her soft skin...since I'd moved inside of her. What was taking so fucking long?

The energy in the air shifted, and I whined before practically running to the door. She was here.

"Ash, what the fuck are you doing?"

"She's here!" I yelled over my shoulder as I raced down the hall.

Her room was all ready. I'd spent hours making sure it was perfect.

I went around the corner and came to a skidding halt when I heard Creed's heavy footsteps...and I smelled my girl—our girl. I could hear her soft breaths. She was sound asleep. Or passed out. Knowing Creed, it could be either.

Seven had followed behind me. "Her hair turned pink," he muttered, before stalking away again.

Her hair had changed colors? That was unexpected.

I'm sure it looked beautiful though, I could picture it in my mind. I knew by tracing her face a thousand times as I'd fucked her that she was the most beautiful girl in existence. Even more beautiful than...no, I wouldn't think about her.

Creed was almost to the closed door of her bedroom, and I hurried to open it up so he could carry her in.

I'd had our staff build her a giant bed with black silken sheets and it was now centered in the room against the wall. He walked over to it and laid her down softly.

We both stared at her, entranced as her chest moved up and down and soft breaths puffed out of her mouth.

I was fucking hard just being near her.

"So I guess it went well," I murmured.

He huffed quietly. "It may have taken a turn there at the end. She may not be the happiest when she wakes up." His tail tapped on the floor behind us, belying his agitation and annoyance.

Well, that wouldn't do. I'd have to turn her frown upside down, or whatever it was that humans said. I wanted to make our girl the happiest she could ever dream of being. She was everything to me...to us.

She just didn't know it yet.

"The pink hair's hot," I commented.

"It happened the second we entered the realm. Hopefully that's the only change that happens as a result of us crossing realms," Creed murmured, his gaze locked on the sleeping beauty in front of us.

The alarms from the outer gates chose that moment to go off, and Blake moaned softly in her sleep. We both froze.

"You've got to be fucking kidding me," Creed growled, casting one more longing glance at Blake before stalking towards the door.

"Third time this week one of them has tried to get through the gates," I helpfully informed him, although I had no intention of going with him to help with the problem.

I had a new job now, and that was to make sure that Blake had everything she ever wanted or needed. I'd never been more excited.

I walked with Creed to the door and listened as he prowled down the hall, spotting the shadow of my brother's monstrous form lurking nearby, the chains that dragged behind him clinking together as he shifted in place.

What a fucking pussy. He was going to be all morose and moody for as long as he could, convinced Blake could never want someone with seven demons living inside of him.

He'd eventually come around. He knew exactly what it felt like to be between Blake's legs...and in her mouth. I'd give him a week—maybe two days actually. And then he'd be begging for her touch just like the rest of us.

I for one wasn't going to waste the opportunity to have Blake with me all the time. I turned around and stalked back into the room, determined to just sit and watch Blake sleeping if that was all I could get right now.

It would still be better than anything else.

Chapter 6

Creed

"You fucking sonofabitch," I growled, clasping my side where the beast's horn had caught me and tore fabric and flesh alike. It stung deep under my ribs, feeling like claws had ripped me apart. I curled my long tail around my waist to maintain pressure against the wound and stop the bleeding. At least for now.

Thirty feet away, the reptilian-like beast unleashed an ungodly screeching howl that flooded our blood-red sky. The sun was descending—the time when these Gazen were most active near the city.

I'd let this one sneak up on me, which was infuriating—especially when I'd been hunting it. The Gazen were crafty bastards with tiny brains, but bodies ten times that of mine. They were made to hunt, and the problem was that lately, they'd been encroaching closer and closer to our city walls. Either attempting to break through our gates, or burrowing deep under the sand, slamming into our underground wall to break through.

They'd been starving out here in the dry-lands surrounding our city, Wyld. We were its main source of food, and as king, my men and I were the protectors in our kingdom to keep us safe from them. The warriors to defend our city.

Boom...boom...boom...

I stiffened.

There it came again, throwing itself in and out of the sand like an enormous worm with clawed feet. It plowed deep, then threw itself back up. Curved horns broke the surface, tossing sand everywhere in an explosion.

A gaping lesion, dripping with green blood, caught my attention across its breastbone from where I'd sliced its leathery skin. Too bad that wouldn't be enough to end it; in order to kill these things, you needed to destroy its brain, or gut it. Otherwise, forget it.

Its mouth gaped open, flashing two rows of sharp teeth, flooding the night with another screech.

Then it vanished, gone under the sand once more. Fuck. Any second now, it would pop out and be on me.

I pulled out my poison-tipped long blade, my fingers running along the ridges of the ivory hilt. And then I grasped the sharp end of the knife between my fingers, careful not to touch the tip dipped in venom. Knees bent, weapon raised, I clenched my teeth, trying to ignore the pain at my side.

I had one chance at this, or I was gone.

Fuck, I lived for this.

Sweat dripped down my spine from the heat of the pain at my side.

Suddenly, the Gazen exploded out of the sand, feet from me, mouth wide, slit eyes filled with vengeance. The thing soared high, towering over me like a mammoth animal about to rain down all its fury on me.

Heart pounding, I hurled my arm forward and released the knife. It spun, whistling through the air, locking in on its target.

Splat.

It hit the creature's one eye, sinking deep down to the hilt. Fuck yes.

Ear-piercing screeches deafened me, and I grinned–I did love the sound of its pitiful cries.

I lunged forward with no time to waste, darting lightning-fast towards the struggling creature.

I threw myself right under its belly–its weak point. I seized another blade from my belt and grasped it with two hands, pushing my arms upward. And in my rush underneath the creature, I sliced the great beast from belly to groin.

Without pause, I wrenched myself out from under and ran from its side, grimacing at how revolting the thing stunk.

Heaving for breath, I twisted around a bit too fast and a sharpness shot up right into my armpit. I groaned, pressing a palm against my ribs. I healed fast, so I'd survive, but it still hurt like a bitch. Couldn't say the same for the Gazen slumped on the sand in a pool of its own green blood and guts.

Disgusting creatures that were too common in our world, breeding uncontrollably. If we had the resources, I'd put together a culling team. But it would have to wait. Our population in the city had been weak from a lack of food, meaning our city walls weren't being regularly reinforced to ensure no breaches.

But that was about to change. I'd make sure of it.

I took a wide berth around the dead beast's head, where its forked tongue had rolled out of its mouth.

By tomorrow, the carcass would be gone. Either eaten by other vermin living outside the walls, or some desperate fucks from within the city who'd sneak out here to harvest its horns and leather pelt.

I climbed up to the creature's head to retrieve my blade so it didn't end up on the dark markets. Our weapons were sought after and sold for ridiculous amounts because they were considered collector's items as a memory of the old Kingdom.

A time when everyone served our queen and followed her religiously. She'd kept order, kept our people safe.

My men and I had sworn our allegiance and loyalty to her. That included having regular sex with our queen.

The lust energy we created fed every monster in our city.

During her reign, our city was at the height of its leadership in the realm. Wyld had once been a prosperous place, one revered by everyone in our Shadowburn realm.

Of course, that kind of success also bred jealousy.

The kind that led to the brutal death of our queen.

She hadn't been the most empathetic queen and she'd had a dark streak, but she didn't deserve to end up dead on her throne, decapitated.

Her killer had wanted us to find her that way. He'd most likely watched our reaction, which told me whoever it was, they enjoyed the chaos and seeing others lose their shit.

I clenched my jaw, having imagined dozens of scenarios of how I'd torture the bastard responsible for her death. I wanted them to scream, to cry, to beg me, and then I'd show them real violence. And they'd wish they were never born.

Her death had been the worst day in the history of our kingdom. We'd lost our queen and our food supply. Unable to find anything equivalent since then, our kingdom has slipped into its downfall ever since.

Those in the city lost hope, some turning feral out of pure desperation and panic.

Slowly, my men and I have regained some sense of peace in the city, but it was nowhere close to what we had before.

She'd been called the Red Queen, because she was born on an auspicious night where both our moons were red. And heartbreakingly, the red moons reappeared on the night of her death. Every red moon, a celebration was held in her honor to help remind everyone that we were still a united kingdom.

Shaking away the past, I refocused on the Gazen's head. I grabbed my knife and wrenched it out of its eye, the sucking sound it made was nausea-inducing.

I leapt down from the beast's shoulder and made a perfect landing in the sand. I cleaned my blade on its paw and tucked it back on my belt.

Uncoiling my tail from around my waist, I gritted my teeth as more blood dripped from my injury. With my knife, I sliced off the bottom half of my shirt, tearing off a long strip from around my waist. Then I tore off one of my sleeves and folded it over on itself.

I pressed the folded sleeve against the wound before tying the long strip of fabric around my middle to hold it in place. I just needed to stop the bleeding and avoid leaving a trail of blood in my wake for other beasts to track me.

Then I continued my path around the city walls, surveying for more Gazen.

The blood-red sky darkened as the sun slipped farther behind the horizon, while the fifty-foot city wall cast a dark shadow over the sandy landscape. Several guard posts were positioned along the perimeter, but many weren't manned, I noticed... something I'd address.

My thoughts turned to Blake. I'd left her passed out on the bed we'd made just for her. I pictured how beautiful she'd been, and how desperately I wanted to fuck her again. But I also needed to give her time to heal.

Her initial transition from the human realm to ours took at least twenty-four hours for her body to adjust to our environment. Though her body would need a bit more time to get all the way used to our environment.

With each inhale I took, the air smelled like the warm fragrance of her skin. Her scent remained in my nostrils.

A feral, predatory obsession came over me.

She was our property now.

Something she would learn to accept no matter how much she protested.

Just thinking of her delicious body squeezed my chest, and my balls pulled up into me at the memories of how many different ways I'd fucked her. How tight her cunt was... and how I craved more of her.

Fucking her in her dreams was a very different experience to claiming her in real life. The sensations were stronger, the energies extraordinary.

I shook my head, trying to get a hold of myself. I'd made a promise to never fall so deep for someone again that I felt like death had taken me if I lost them.

The pain from losing our queen still hummed within me, something I'd grieved and accepted long ago. Except, once pain etched into your soul, it stayed with you for life.

All those emotions I forbade myself had surged through me the moment I had Blake in my arms. They rushed at me, promising to swallow and drown me.

Thinking of her was like someone touching live wires to my nerves. It jolted through me, reminding me of her every second of the day.

Every inch of her was drop-dead gorgeous, and I knew that already I'd let myself go too far with how obsessed I'd become.

A sudden screech sliced through the air, stealing me from my thoughts.

My ears perked up.

It came from up ahead.

Another Gazen? Fuck.

I pushed into a run over the fine sand, holding a hand to my side, and hurried up. The city was enormous, so it made sense to always hunt in pairs to cover more ground. Especially if you needed backup.

Let's hope Seven hasn't been ambushed by two beasts.

Curving around the wall, Seven came into view. Even in the dim light, he blended into the night with his black clothes, hood, and the mask covering the bottom half of his face. The only thing he showed were his violet eyes.

A Gazen burst out of the sand feet from him, and he backpedaled, telling me he wasn't expecting it that close. To be fair, this Gazen was a motherfucking monster, bigger than the one I'd just fought.

I sprinted forward, the wind ripping through my hair, my tail whipping behind me.

Seven threw himself up, barely missing being skewered by the animal's twisted horns. He crashed onto its back. Seven moved like a storm, but one wrong move and he'd end up with more than an injury like mine.

My men were the only family I had, and I had no intention of losing any of them. No matter how much they pissed me off most days.

Coming up behind the beast, it bucked and looked ready to dive back into the sand, and I gave out a low whistle to Seven.

He glanced up, spotting me coming up fast.

A nod was all he gave me, and he threw himself onto the creature's head, needing to reach its eye.

Making excellent pace, I lunged myself forward, lowering my head, shoulders stiff, and I rammed straight into its stumpy rear. My horns pierced the leather hide and sank right into flesh.

I shoved my hands against the beast and pulled free before it kicked back. Throwing myself out of reach, I rolled and leapt back up, just as the beast swung his huge head in my direction.

"Come at me, motherfucker," I yelled.

Seven lost his balance but grasped onto its horn, and

swung from them wildly. It was almost laughable if we weren't dealing with a blood-thirsty beast.

"Stop swinging around," I yelled at him mockingly.

He growled and scrambled back up over the Gazen's head before showing me the finger.

I burst out laughing as he fought to hold on just as the damned thing was about to dive underground.

"Seven," I bellowed, stepping forward as the creature bucked with him holding onto its horns. "Get this done already or you're going under."

He didn't reply but threw himself over the frame of the animal's huge brow, bringing down his blade, and slammed it dead center into his eye.

Bucking upward, Seven was thrown backward, and I chased after him as he hit the sand. Snatching him by the arm, I heaved him to his feet and dragged him from the beast going ballistic as it died.

"Didn't need your help," he barked in the same pissy look he always wore. He wiped his hands down his legs then fixed the mask that had slipped under his nose.

"Never said you did," I muttered, while we both watched the Gazen plummet to the ground with a heaved breath. Dead. "But I've never seen you so slow in your kill before."

He eyed my wound and torn shirt. "By the looks of it, you didn't fare too well yourself." Vein-like ridges formed across the bridge of his nose from his scowl. His agitation was rubbing me the wrong way.

"Let's walk," I commanded, huffing in frustration.

He sprinted over to the creature to retrieve his blade, then we made the long trek around the city, surveying for more creatures.

"She's so much more beautiful in real life," he said unexpectedly, and at first I assumed he hadn't meant to say those words out loud. Of course, I knew instantly who he was referring to.

"Her beauty's easy to become transfixed by," I muttered. "I know you're pining for her."

"Are you insinuating that I'm jealous? Fuck you, Creed," he growled, making a strange face. Most likely realizing how irrationally he responded to a simple comment. "I'm eager to get our chance to meet her in person, to taste her, to feed. I can smell her on you. It's so strong, it's making my head dizzy." His eyes lit up with a desperate flame when he spoke of her.

"You're right, she's ours," I reminded him, holding back my anger, aware that my three men have been anxiously waiting for her arrival. They fed on the lust energy I generated when I fucked her. And seeing how we'd been enjoying her in dreams for the last couple of years, I might not have been the only one who'd developed an unhealthy obsession with Blake during that time.

"Next time, we join you. We don't get left out," he commanded, the outline of his body darkening.

A beat of silence passed between us, then with a loud exhale and droop of his shoulders, he decided to double down his aggression. "It's been so long since we've fed outside a dream."

"That it has been," I muttered, my lips curling over teeth at his earlier uncouth manner.

Seven was always an unpredictable asshole. The one who caught you off guard because each day you had no idea who you were going to be dealing with.

He was furious one day, sly the next, rude and hostile another, depressed another, but jealousy was new for him. His personalities varied, and I was convinced I'd met all seven of his demons, but today he surprised me.

While the tide of his emotions rising sharply from him had

been unexpected, it left me mulling over whether the other men felt the same.

Desperate.

Jealous.

Furious.

Most likely, I decided.

"When she wakes up, we'll share a meal with her to introduce her to us in a peaceful environment," I stated abruptly. "She'll be startled, and everything is new to her. We take it slowly. No trouble, or terrifying her."

"She's in Wyld, surrounded by monsters." He rolled his eyes. "She'll have to get used to it soon enough."

I grumbled under my breath, and a moment later, Seven reluctantly nodded. "Don't worry," he reassured me brusquely. "I won't kill anyone at the dinner table. Not after how pissed you got last time."

He avoided my stare when I glared at him, reminded of him killing the ambassador of the closest city in our realm, which could have easily ignited a war between us.

War at a time when we were at our weakest.

The damage was done though.

Of course, I didn't believe him to keep his word. But as long as he kept his crazy away from Blake for a short while, I didn't give a fuck who he took out.

Chapter 7

Blake

I once read somewhere that we were all angels before we became demons.

For some reason, as I laid in a bed that carried Creed's scent, staring up at the black ceiling, that quote came to mind. Did that mean that the monsters had once been angels as well?

Considering the things they'd done to me in my dreams, it seemed highly unlikely.

I was almost embarrassed to admit how my body still hummed from how hard he fucked me back in my apartment. How much I enjoyed it.

And that was the problem, wasn't it? I shouldn't have found anything sexy about such a beast, only repulsion. But just like in my dreams, he did things to me I couldn't deny. For so long, I'd been alone, and their visits at night became the one consistent thing in my life I could rely on.

Still, it didn't change the fact that Creed was pure sin. And I craved him because I must be weak.

But that left me with the question of where in the world was I now?

Slowly, I pushed myself out of the enormous bed covered in black sheets and sat on the edge of the mattress until the room stopped turning.

Bright light poured into the room through the wraparound window that spanned two walls, giving the black stone walls a shimmering glint. The wall behind the bed resembled an archeological discovery of a partially unearthed skeleton. Except whatever that was, it had four legs and enormous wings with a long-snouted nose. It gave me the creeps.

My feet touched the cold, wooden floor as I got up. There was no other furniture in this room, just the bed that took up most of the space, and three immense black doors. I made my way to the smaller door across from the bed, which had to be the entry.

I pushed down on the handle. Locked. The worry in my gut deepened.

On bare feet, I walked briskly to the window and glanced out to what looked like an ocean of sand. Was I in a desert?

I gasped at first, just trying to make sense of it all. The sky held blue and red tones, and the sun was especially bright. So much so that I squinted against its light.

Glancing down from the window was impossible from my angle. My attempt to open the window failed miserably as my muscles strained, and I gave up.

Turning back around, I found a dress neatly folded up on the end of the bed.

But first, I moved to another door which opened up to an enormous walk-in wardrobe.

I might have drooled over the sheer size of the room, but it was empty of clothing.

I retreated to the last door which revealed a bathroom. Black opal tiles with streaks of blues and golds ran from the doorway to an open shower with three showerheads.

My gaze immediately fell to the floor-to-ceiling windows

to my left, revealing more of the sand landscape. I gasped, unable to believe my eyes at the expansive view.

There were no blinds either.

Glancing back at the shower, I hesitated. I took a whiff of myself and scrunched up my nose, so I grabbed a folded towel from the shelves and shut the door.

Something bright caught my attention in the mirror above the sink just as I twisted back into the room.

A small cry fell from my lips, and I dropped my towel as I stared at myself. Wait! That couldn't be me. I rushed over to the mirror, my hands pulling at my *now* pink hair.

Pink hair!

My eyes bulged at the sight. I'd always had black hair, and I think I would have remembered dyeing it.

This had to be some mistake. The more I studied myself, the more that dizzying sensation overwhelmed me.

Checking my roots closely, the color had been perfectly blended to appear natural. Why would someone dye my hair while I slept? Looking back, I had to admit, the pink did suit my pale complexion...but that wasn't the point.

I blinked at the shower once more, then at the wall made of glass. "Who's going to see me this high up anyway?" I murmured to myself, and in no time, I stripped and rushed under the hot spray, figuring the color in my hair was some terrible joke someone played on me, and I'd wash it out. Plus, the water might wake me up from this nightmare.

I moaned as hot water pelted against my body from three jets, and I stayed there for a long while, just letting it wash over me. Lately, nothing made sense; I wondered if I was dreaming right now.

Creed's words came to mind. *I'm afraid, Pet, that it's not an option for you to be anywhere but with me.*

Grabbing a black bottle of what smelled and looked like

shampoo on my fingers, I lathered my hair, figuring pink dye washed out of hair easily.

Then I scrubbed my whole body with it, becoming a white marshmallow of suds.

By the time I finished and dried off, I felt somewhat normal and stood in front of the mirror wrapped in a white towel.

My hair was still pink. I shook my head, my chest tightening. How could I not remember how my hair changed color?

Using a wide-toothed comb from the drawer, I ran it through my hair, deciding the color was the least of my problems.

I grabbed the dress from the bed and slipped it over my head. The fabric was like liquid and cascaded down my body in waves, feeling like silk against my skin.

I moved back into the bathroom to glance at myself, surprised at how perfectly the black dress fit. With short sleeves and a soft, sweeping breast line, it followed every curve, outlining the shape of my breasts, my nipples pressing against the fabric. There were slits on both sides, hitting high up on my thighs.

This dress needed underwear badly, but of course, I found none. Now to get out of the room. I frantically checked all the drawers in the bathroom for a pin or anything to trip the lock.

Just as I shut a drawer, the sound of the front door to the bedroom opening caught my attention. I paused and twisted around, my heart striking my ribcage.

Was it Creed?

A shadow fell over the bathroom entranceway, then someone slithered in full view of the walk-in wardrobe. Okay, scratch that. Not someone... more like something.

A gray glob monster slid forward, and I shrank back involuntarily, my hip hitting the sharp edge of the sink. The creature had no real neck, but goo just flowed downward from its smooth, round head to the floor in a cascading motion.

Eyes bright as the sun blinked at me, nostrils flaring while bits of glob dripped over its thin lips.

I couldn't breathe, let alone say one word.

"I am Freddy, Creed's number one," he announced in a snarky voice, which was not what I expected. "Come with me. The King awaits you on the balcony."

It took me several attempts to find my voice, carefully trying not to look as shocked as I felt on the inside. I was talking to a glob.

When I didn't respond, he said, "I see you found the dress I ordered for you."

Glancing down and back up, I was half tempted to ask him for a pair of underwear, but I stopped myself, wondering if that was the kind of information you asked a blob monster. The guy didn't have any legs, which also explained why I had no shoes with this outfit.

"Nice to meet you, Freddy, I'm Blake," I finally said, sounding way too formal, but my nerves were dancing across my temples and I wasn't exactly thinking straight.

He didn't respond but slithered across the room and out the door. I hurried after him for the simple reason that I had to see Creed and work out how to return home.

Following Freddy proved to be a mistake when you were barefoot because, like a slug, he left behind a thin line of clear slime. My feet slipped from under me, but by some miracle, I caught myself.

I quickly moved to stand by his side once out in the hallway.

Overhead, there was a glass dome, flooding the hall with natural light. Three fish tanks that resembled upright coffins lined the wall. Inside them were some strange-looking plants that almost took on a humanoid shape. My skin crawled because I could swear they watched me.

Were those eyes? I inched closer and a round shrub for a head twisted to look at me, its leaves swaying in the water akin to hair.

I flinched backward, my heel sliding on Freddy's slime, and in my stumble, I crashed my back against the wall. Shit. My heart raced wildly.

Freddy's head twisted to look at me up against the wall, while his body didn't move in a freaky demon-possessed move.

"Keep up." Then he continued gliding along the hallway to the doors that opened to reveal an elevator.

"Where are we exactly?" I hurried to join him, staying away from the slime.

"You're in the city of Wyld, one of the most elite cities in the realm of Shadowburn." He grinned, revealing a row of extremely sharp teeth, definitely managing to look like a serial killer.

The hairs on my nape lifted.

I entered the elevator with him against my better judgment, biting on my lip as anxiety danced up my spine, but I couldn't hide in my room forever either.

Freddy spoke the word firmly, "Balcony," and a raspy voice from with the walls confirmed by repeating, *balcony*. I flinched, convinced a monster was operating the elevator.

Then next thing I knew, we were suddenly lurching sideways.

I gripped onto the wall to stop myself from falling over.

Freddy looked at me, giving me his toothy smile again, and I grimaced on the inside.

My heart was pounding too hard to really pay attention to him talking about how old the tower we were in was.

"When you said realm before, what country is that exactly?" I asked, hopeful this was some crazy misunderstanding.

He laughed at me, sounding like he might be choking. "You aren't on earth. I told you already, this is Shadowburn, our home world. But you'll get used to it."

I instantly wanted to cry at his words because I didn't want to get used to it. This wasn't my home.

The elevator doors slid open to bright light. I stepped out into a foyer quickly, and the doors shut behind me. I turned to find Freddy had abandoned me.

Okay, fine. So I guessed Creed was out here and he had a lot of explaining to do.

My attention swept to the open glass doors that lead to a balcony made of red sandstone. It curved outward on either side of me, appearing to circle around the building.

I paused as soon as my gaze landed on the sight in front of me.

I definitely wasn't on earth. I couldn't be.

All I saw was the view beyond the decorative metal railing, and my mouth fell open. I stumbled forward, convinced I had to be dreaming.

It was a chaotic city that had to come straight out of Hell.

Dozens upon dozens of towers resembling alien pods from movies filled an enormous area that kept on going and going in every direction. Blacks and grays, the structures blended in with hundreds of open bridges that arched from one tower to the next. One building in front of us had at least four levels of bridges spanning outward, joined to the other buildings nearby.

They were arteries, all connected like a circulatory system.

The reddish tinge of the sun burned against the gold in the buildings. When I glanced farther down over the balcony, I couldn't see where it ended...all that lay there were masses of bridges and darkness. Though an oppressive heat rose upward, hitting my face as though I stood over a furnace.

I pulled back to escape the immediate heat, having no idea

how anyone could stand being in that burning temperature for too long.

A shadow cast over me, and I craned my neck up to see several large birds circling overhead. Every now and then, one swooped down into the city, re-emerging moments later with something huge in its talons.

God, was it eating the monsters?

Perspiration ran down my temple, and I wiped my brow with the back of my hand, unsure what I was seeing, to be honest.

So many voices came from the people on the balconies and bridges in front of me, the sound bubbling into a deafening chatter. The closer I looked, the more I noticed they weren't people after all. Just like the monsters in my dreams, they were terrifying and hideous beings.

A shiver raced up my spine at the startling realization that I was in an actual monstrous world. There was no way that my mind could have come up with this scene in front of me.

This was fucking real.

Goosebumps traveled up my arms.

Was this how Dorothy felt in Wizard of Oz? Completely overwhelmed, confused, and terribly scared that she'd die in Oz–except replace all the cute singing munchkins with terrifying nightmarish monsters.

"You're finally awake, Pet," a deep voice rasped behind me.

Before I even turned to face him, my knees wobbled slightly at the sound of his delicious voice.

Creed loomed in front of me in his monster form, standing close to eight feet tall. A tingling burst through my stomach at seeing him, which was wrong considering I was also annoyed and confused.

Horns glinting in the sunlight, piercing red eyes, and those sharp fangs I'd felt on my flesh now cushioned on his lower lip,

Creed awakened something within me that left me pining for him.

I was complicated and incredibly messed up apparently.

Creed wore black pants and a buttoned-up jacket, looking ready to rush into a battlefield. His hair fluttered in the breeze, falling messily around his face.

When he reached a hand out for me, I stepped back and sucked in a raspy breath. "You took me from my home."

"This is now your home, and I'm not going to hurt you," he explained, his outstretched hand still between us, palm upward, fingers extending. When he stared at me, it seemed his eyes were boring right into my soul with a possessiveness I was coming to crave.

This monster could bring me unimaginable pleasure–I knew that–but the thought of me being here to feed him and his monsters was terrifying.

When I didn't take his hand, he closed the distance between us, staring out over the expansive city. Being this close to him, in the shadow of his towering body, wasn't unpleasant...it was rather alarmingly enjoyable actually. But it didn't ease the anger coiling in my chest that I'd been ripped out of my life–as shitty of a life as it had been.

"Everyone living in the city has been waiting for a solution that you offer," he said in a matter-of-fact tone. "They've been desperate and scared for a long time."

His explanations back in my apartment grazed my mind about how our lust fed his kingdom, how he and his men having sex with me supplied their city with enough energy to sate them all.

"What if that's not what I want?" The sight of the enormous city and how many monsters relied on lust energy to feed left me uneasy.

Was this what I wanted? To end up as the monsters' sex slave?

His twisted brow, together with a piercing gaze, lent itself to a sinfully crafted scowl only Creed could pull off.

He unceremoniously drew me toward him roughly, one clawed hand on the back of my head, the other at my hip. He leaned in closer so we were face to face, and desire instantly burst within me. His scent screamed sex, and all my thoughts fell on his strong jaw and those perfect lips.

My body softened, and it didn't matter how much my mind screamed to pull away from the monster—my body fell prey.

There was no pause in the way he kissed me either. He claimed me savagely with his mouth, tongue, and fangs. They pierced my lips, then he delicately licked my blood with longer strokes.

I should have been horrified. I should have pushed him away. Instead, a low rumble of need hummed deep in my core. I leaned closer, my clit pulsing, and I fought the urge to moan out loud. It still surprised me how my body reacted to his touches.

His hand dipped to my rear, stroking me in tight little circles, the pinch of his nails easily felt through the thin fabric of my dress.

"I smell your desire," he growled, while grinding himself against me. "You're beautiful, beyond any of my expectations. There's no question of whether you want to help us. I've made you mine."

My cheeks flushed with opposing emotions that tore me apart. The flutter in my stomach from being called beautiful for the first time in my life, to his admittance that I was stuck here.

And something was definitely wrong with me to be this ridiculously turned on by a monster.

His actions were outright dominant. His claws moved

down my thigh, finding the slit in my dress, and quickly his fingers climbed underneath to settle on my ass.

A moan slipped past my lips at the touch–at the way his claws dug into flesh.

He laughed at me. "I'm obsessed with how responsive your body is to me."

My breath caught in my lungs, and I balanced on the edge of losing myself. It came so easily around Creed when he seized control over me. "You do things to me that I can't control."

"That's not me, Pet. That's your body calling me to fuck you."

"But this is so much more than in my dreams. I can't explain it."

Creed smirked, a forked tongue sweeping across his lower lip, seeming to approve of my reaction to him.

Darkness circled behind his eyes. Would he take me now? Out on the balcony? The thought left me enveloped in heat, and Creed knew exactly how he made me feel. His smile said it all. And I hated him for it.

He glanced over my shoulder, and I turned my head to follow his line of sight toward the city.

"Can you see it?" he said.

Tiny heat waves rippled across the air.

They vanished as quickly as they came. And suddenly, several beastly monsters in the nearest tower were cheering loudly, waving up, then screaming, "More."

"Did we just feed them?" I gasped aloud, still unsure how the feeding physically worked.

"Barely," he answered. "It was the equivalent of letting you inhale the smell of your favorite meal."

I blinked back at the monsters who were like ants from up here, yet they'd picked up on our momentary kiss. I couldn't ignore the sense of satisfaction such an act brought me, which of course made no sense.

"When do I get to go home?" I asked abruptly, turning back toward him.

"*This* is your home now, Pet. I promise you that you will find beauty in our world that will bring you the kind of joy you never found back on earth. I will make it my mission to give you everything you'll ever want."

I swallowed hard, not sure I agreed. Nothing in this world felt welcoming or like home.

"It's time for you to eat something and meet the others," Creed said, changing the topic quickly.

He collected my hand into his large clawed one. My hand vanished inside his, miniature in comparison. He moved with long strides which had me needing to walk twice as fast just to keep up with him.

Nerves knotted in my gut at the thought of meeting the others, considering how things had turned out between Creed and me so far.

Around the corner of the balcony, a round table came into view along with three other monsters sitting there, watching us eagerly.

I recognized them immediately from my dreams. It was a strange sensation to meet up with someone for the first time after having already experienced my most intimate moments with them. These monsters claimed my virginity, they took it all, and now they looked at me like I was their savior.

My gaze roamed over each of the monsters frantically because normally when you saw creatures like these, you screamed and ran. Except, I was about to join them as a sense of familiarity filled me. Which confirmed how completely broken I was.

I stood near the chair Creed pulled out for me, frozen, speechless.

Standing in front of them left me both terrified and bashful.

Did I mention I was complicated?

"Have you been a good girl for me, Blake?" the most hideous of monsters murmured, sitting across the large table from me, head back, sniffing the air. He was what nightmares were made of.

Muscles rippling under his leathery skin. Clawed hands that could rip me in half. But the most terrifying thing was his head... a large mouth without lips that were all teeth, stretching the width of his face, and huge curled horns that came out from the sides of his head.

And yet, I knew from my dreams that he was my most tender lover.

We stared at each other for a long pause, and a blend of emotions played in my chest–desire, longing, fear, and unease.

"I'm always good," I answered, maybe a bit too flirty considering the situation.

He licked his teeth, grinning creepily, which I strangely didn't find repulsive.

"Let me officially introduce you to my circle," Creed said as he stared at me. At the calmness in his voice, I released the pent-up anguish I'd been holding onto.

"In front of you is Ash. To your right is his twin, Seven, and to the left is Tempest. Now, sit," Creed ordered me, and I slipped into the seat.

They smiled and gave me their greetings in unison, which almost made me laugh. "How did I not know you two were twins?" I asked instead.

"Because I'm the handsome one," Ash growled, lifting his chin in an almost comical manner.

Seven simply rolled his eyes. All I saw of him were his piercing eyes. He wore all black. Clothes, hood, and a mask covering the bottom half of his face...nothing about him screamed human. The energy he gave out was practically hostile.

Especially when I noticed his long fingers that extended into claws. He never removed his clothes completely when he claimed me in my dreams, only his face mask and heavy cock, but his lips were the most sensual I'd ever felt on my skin.

Though between the four monsters, he confused me the most as he behaved differently each time he turned up in my dreams, even down to the way we had sex. I never really knew what to expect with him.

"Wait. Where's her food?" Creed interrupted, staring at the monsters, to which no one answered. They were too busy gawking at me, and I felt their eyes on me all over, my skin burning up.

Creed huffed and called out for Freddy, then marched away, leaving me alone with them.

"You're creeping her out, Ash, with that smile. So many teeth," Seven blurted, almost vengefully.

"Fuck you, Seven," Ash snarled, and every bone in my body shivered at his booming voice. "You leering at her is freaking her out."

"You'll get used to their bickering," Tempest interrupted. His eyes were slits like that of a serpent. The rest of his body resembled a shadow. Dark, lengthy teeth and horns, the edges of his body fraying. When the sunlight hit him, it almost seemed to travel right through his body.

He was the one who'd stayed in the shadows. I knew him extremely well because he was always a bit too rough with me, and liked to remind me what a dirty whore I was as he took me.

He leaned in closer. "You've been on my mind endlessly, little human. Thinking about how you love it when I lick your ass and you scream for more. I missed you."

My cheeks flushed immediately at how candidly he talked

when it felt as though I had no control of myself in my dreams.

"Is that the first thing you say when meeting her?" Ash griped, his broad shoulders rising. "Show some fucking respect."

Tempest shrugged and grinned at me. "I know you loved it. I'm not embarrassed."

"Neither am I," I answered bravely. "But I'm also trying to not pass out from so many new things being thrown at me."

"See, you're being a prick," Ash barked at Tempest. "Back the fuck off." He inched forward on his seat, and for a moment, I thought he might pick me up in his arms and steal me away from the others. I couldn't say I'd be unhappy with that decision.

They were too much, and all I could think was, what had I gotten myself into?

Ash's body started shimmering. In the blink of an eye, gone was the monster, replaced with a god. It was the best way to describe him, and he had me flushing with heat each time I saw his human form in my dreams.

I gasped, unsure I could get used to how easily they shifted.

Dark hair sat unkempt around his face, shaved short around the sides and back. A lock of hair always swept across one eye that I adored. Sharp cheekbones, and eyes so pale blue that they were almost milky white. He wore a deep chocolate-colored shirt, sleeves rolled to his elbows, and might have just walked off a runway.

"Is this better?" he almost purred, smiling wickedly.

"Very much so," I answered.

He then poked Tempest in the arm. "Don't be a fuckhead. Change."

Tempest didn't respond right away, but fell silent, giving me a chilling smile. In a flash, he changed into his human form too, and I almost fell off my chair at how remarkably handsome he was. He rarely took human form during my dreams, and I never understood why when his looks stole my breath.

He had the face of an angel, carved out of stone, striking emerald eyes, and a square jawline with a light shadow of growth. Dressed casually in navy-colored pants and a Henley top, he looked unimpressed.

"Your turn, Seven," Tempest barked, his voice full of irritation and mockery.

Seven didn't move but the air thickened, his glare darkening, and I expected him to fly across the table and wring Tempest's neck. I'd never seen Seven as anything but the way he looked now in my dreams. Perhaps he had no other form.

"Well, this is fun," I murmured, noticing Creed making his way toward us. "I finally get to see what your personalities are really like." I looked around nervously as every eye remained trained on me. Seven was intense and broody. Tempest appeared to be in a dickhead mood, while Ash grinned at me deviously from across the table.

What a great team we made.

Creed pulled up a chair next to me. He glanced around at every one of the men, raising an eyebrow.

"Hopefully you three have made her feel welcome."

Before anyone could respond, Freddy rushed over to us, pushing a small food trolley with a squeaky wheel, and looking pissed for a blob monster.

"Sorry for the delay," he grumbled at me, placing several plates of food in front of me along with a big glass of water, before slithering out of there.

"Eat," Creed insisted.

I looked at the four bowls, each one of them filled to the brim with green salad leaves and purple slices of a vegetable I didn't recognize. In fact, aside from the leaves, I had no idea what was in the bowls, most of all what the small blue orbs were. But it smelled like French dressing, and my stomach grumbled with hunger. My mouth watered too, no matter how bland the food looked.

"These vegetables are grown in our greenhouse," Creed explained. "They're safe for you to eat."

Not finding a fork, and with the way Freddy eyed me like I got him into trouble, I didn't want to create an enemy on my first day. So I picked at the lettuce first with my fingers, nibbling on it. It tasted normal. The blue globes were exactly like tomatoes, so I dug in, surprised at how starved I was.

"Why do you grow human food?" I asked between bites, noting everyone watched me intensely. Had they never seen someone eat before?

"Our scientists are experimenting with different vegetation from Earth that contains a lot of minerals we hoped might produce natural energies for our feeding," Ash explained, then licked his lips as I took another bite of my salad, his mouth almost mimicking mine.

"You might be hard to feed, Pet," Creed confessed. "Especially since humans need protein and we only have salads for you. I've assigned Freddy with the task of finding you other things to eat."

Oh, great. A glob monster was going to find me food. I was slightly scared.

"What about a Gazen?" Tempest offered. "They have lots of meat on them and we kill enough of them." He reclined in his seat, arms draped by his side, and despite talking to Creed, he never stopped looking at me.

My heart was beating fast against my ribcage under their gazes.

"They're filthy things that live in the sand," Ash responded. "She is not eating those vermin. Only the best for our Blake."

Ash was melting my heart with how sweet he was. This

gorgeous man with hazy white eyes kept protecting me, and I adored him for that.

"The avis could work," Seven suggested. "We have enough of them flying over our city attacking locals, and I do believe humans love to eat birds, right?" He looked at me with a raised eyebrow.

"Chicken mostly," I murmured, glancing at him with a smile he never returned. "That's what we eat lots of back home."

"I'll send Freddy to catch several avis for you," Creed confirmed, and I had no idea how the blob monster was supposed to do that or what an avis bird was, but I kept on eating my salad.

The monsters' conversation heated up on various topics of conversation of what might be edible for me. Out of all the monsters, I appreciated how Ash and Creed stood up for me while Tempest suggested things that sounded disgusting. He was a sadist, wasn't he? Though part of me wondered if he was attempting to get a rise out of me.

I lifted my gaze to Seven and how intensely he studied me, keeping mostly quiet.

My hands started to sweat with his eyes on me. His expression gave nothing away. He was a blank page, and all that went through my mind was our last time together in my dream. As if sensing my thoughts, that same devious look crossed his face now as it had back then.

"Strip," he demanded. "I need you naked."

I hesitated for a second, which was too much time to wait for this monster apparently. He growled, his hand tugging his huge cock from his pants. He palmed it, the thick ridges running the length of his long shaft bringing me insane pleasure when we had fucked. I hitched a breath all the way down to my lungs at the sight of how thick and ready he was.

"I told you to take your clothes off." His other clawed hand

shredded my dress to pieces with two deft moves, leaving me completely naked. I gasped at how much he enjoyed making me startle.

"You may be the sexiest thing I've seen, but you will obey me. Now, lay back for me, gorgeous. I need to taste that pussy of yours." He lifted me with ease to sit on the edge of the table and brought my legs up before parting them.

I lay back down, quivering with an unbearable need as his attention fell on my swollen, slick flesh. In my mind, I told myself I should resist him and not enjoy him as much as I had been. Except with arousal rippling through me, excitement twisting me inside out, I stood no chance at pushing him away.

"Such a beautiful cunt," he purred. "I've thought of nothing else but you since last night." He gently brushed the knuckles of his fingers across my sensitive folds, prying them open. "You're so swollen for me. I love how fucking turned on you are." He rubbed my clit in tight circles as he spoke, teasing me relentlessly.

Shadows crowded in around me, and even without seeing their faces, I knew the other three monsters watched. They always watched.

I trembled beneath the monster's touches.

"Is this what you want?" he demanded, towering over me, his form foreboding, ridges across his nose deepening. His clawed hands extended, and he was the monster from my nightmares who brought me to orgasm every night.

"Y-yes please," I managed between gasping breaths.

He dropped to his knees, his clawed hands pressing my legs wider, showing him everything, giving him everything I had.

My breaths came too fast when Seven growled like a predator, his voice raspy, thick with lust. "You're so pink, so wet."

The roar on his throat turned me on ridiculously, and when his scorching hot breath brushed across my wet lips, I panted with desperation.

"I'm going to tongue-fuck you, lick and suck on your pussy,

and we're not going to stop until I take my fill of your sweet cum. I want your honey all over my face, alright?"

The sound that came from my throat might have been a cry for more, but it was hard to tell when I was drowning in arousal. He pressed his lips to my drenched pussy, and that was the moment I lost all control.

The monster was starving, devouring me savagely with his tongue and lips. He was a beast.

I arched my back, crying out. "Yes, just like that. Fuck..."

Every stroke pushed me right to the edge, and I rocked my hips, grinding myself against his face.

Claws dug into my inner thighs, breaking skin, then he pushed his tongue into me. Thick and long, he flicked my insides.

I clasped my eyes shut, the tension building, and I thrashed from how quickly I was about to climax.

Just when I heard a click that sounded like bones cracking, I opened my eyes, startled. I stared down at the monster between my thighs.

His dark eyes were rolling upward. And that's when I noticed him unhinging his jaw.

Suddenly, I felt like a victim in front of a snake about to be devoured. His bones cracked once more, mouth wide, and I should have been scared, but I'd learned a long time ago that these monsters would push me to the limits... anything to make me orgasm so hard that it felt like my world had shattered.

Slick glistened on his mouth and chin, but he didn't waste a second. He pushed his huge mouth against me once more, his thick tongue pressing into my pussy.

Deeper. Deeper.

So much more that I shook uncontrollably, feeling him in regions he'd never reached before. His nose pressed on my clit, and that was when he did things to me that I never thought possible.

The tension became too much, my breathing erratic. Every muscle tightened. I bucked wildly beneath him.

"Oh my god, please don't stop, please..."

"There is no god, Blake," one of the other monsters growled from within the shadows. "Only the things that will fuck you in the dark and worship the ground you step on."

Holding on was close to impossible, his words driving me to the point of no return. In that exact moment that the other monsters stepped forward, staring, waiting for their turn, the orgasm crashed through me like a tidal wave, over and over relentlessly.

My back arched as I screamed, the pleasure wreaking havoc with my body, and somehow I managed to hear the monster's grunts as he lapped up every drop I gave him...

As if sensing my discomfort, the grin in Seven's eyes turned pure evil. Was he feeding on my memory? Was that possible?

I kept on eating as it gave me an excuse to not look at them while unease settled in my bones.

The slithering sound of Freddy returning had me glancing over my shoulder at his approach.

"I'm sorry for the interruption, Master, but there's an urgent matter that needs your attention regarding Gazens. They are back, at least half a dozen."

"Fuck," Creed groaned, his hands fisting by his side. He jerked to his feet. "Seven, Tempest, you're with me. Let's go. Ash, you'll give Blake a safe tour of the city."

"You bet." Ash beamed with excitement.

Creed leaned down at my side, his hand on mine. "Ash will take good care of you, Pet. I'll return as soon as I can."

I didn't get a chance to respond with food still in my mouth, but he and his two men stormed off the balcony with Freddy. I glanced over to Ash who smiled a bit too deviously.

The thing about Ash was that his words dripped with

honey, but when it came to sex, I'd seen him turn feral. And right then, he stared at me with that same hunger that might ruin me.

"We're going to have so much fun," he muttered, and for some reason, his promise sounded like the complete opposite of showing me around the city safely.

Chapter 8

Blake

"I hope they fit," Ash said, standing up from his chair, while a young maid who glowed a violet color and had one cyclops eye, placed a pair of open-toed sandals in front of me. Then she scurried away, keeping her head low, too afraid to even look at me.

Strange behavior, but when I turned back to the shoes, I wanted to kiss Ash for being so considerate and noticing that I wore no footwear. I slipped into the sandals.

"They feel like they were made for me. Thank you so much." I leaned down and tied up the straps.

In truth, I was almost crying because I could count on one hand the amount of people who had ever treated me with such care. And one of them was a monster.

"I'm not used to people being kind to me."

He smiled so beautifully that I easily forgot I was staring at him for too long. I rather enjoyed watching the way the breeze tossed his dark hair out of his face, though when he looked at me with those haunting, milky eyes, they were focused on something over my shoulder. When I checked behind me, there was nothing there.

He approached me with confidence in his stride–he was so goddamn gorgeous, there was no getting used to it. "You deserve the world delivered to you on a platter."

I gushed at his words as his shadows cascaded over me, and underneath his fresh soap smell, I caught his musk scent. He paused impossibly close to me, our arms brushing, sending a jolt of electricity over my skin at how easily he affected me.

"How anyone could not treat you as anything else is beyond me. But that's something you'll never have to worry about now that you're with us."

I pinched my lips to the side, loving the attention but also slightly alarmed at how obsessive he sounded.

But the more I looked up at him, the more I noticed something strange. His eyes weren't focused on mine. They lingered a bit off the mark by a few inches as though he was inspecting my cheek the whole time we spoke.

Curious.

I raised a hand between us and waved it. His pale pupils didn't move. Not once.

He caught me by the wrist mid-air, his long fingers gripping me hard. "What are you doing?"

"Can you actually see me?" I asked, my heart sinking through me at the thought.

He shook his head, which had me drawing in a sharp inhale. "I was born with no sight, but it makes no difference. My smell and hearing are exceptional, so don't pity me, Blake." His voice darkened slightly, and I heard the pride beneath his words.

"I don't pity you. I'm in awe," I responded, my own breaths growing irregular as I tried not to feel sympathy for him. He moved around as if he saw everything, and I was completely impressed. "How could you tell I wore no shoes?" I stared at him quizzically.

"The sound of your bare feet on the stone balcony gave

you away," he answered. "Should we start our tour then?" He offered me his hand, changing the topic, which was fine. It might be a sensitive topic for him.

"While you're with me, no one will so much as look at you. If they touch you, I'll tear heads off," he promised me with a smile.

"I'll hold you to that." I attempted to laugh, but I ended up sounding more like I choked. My nerves were extremely tight and I tried hard to keep it together.

If my time in the asylum had taught me anything, it had been to remain calm even when the world was burning around you. Sure, I was now in an apparent monster world–something I was still trying to come to terms with–but I wasn't going to lose my head until I felt for sure I knew what was going on.

I accepted Ash's hand, and we walked to the rear of the balcony. "I know you're nervous," he said. "Just pretend we're in one of your dreams where I visit you."

That time I did manage to laugh without sounding like a dying cat. "That's the problem. I can't tell if this is real or all in my head."

His hand gave a light squeeze over mine. "Transitioning into our realm will take you a bit of time as your body adjusts. It's why your hair turned pink... a reaction to your body needing to change. But I can promise you that this is very real, Blake."

That was what worried me.

I lifted my attention in front of us where the first thing I saw were two human-sized spiders.

I cried out, my body flailing in my attempt to backpedal–something impossible with Ash holding me tightly by my arm.

"It's alright," he reassured me. "They're guards and are here to protect you."

I shook my head, staring at the arachna-type monsters that

stood tall as Ash at the bridge entrance. Long, hairy spidery legs, with bulbous, black bodies, they had a streak of red across their almost humanoid heads. Six eyes and a wide mouth.

They watched us, all the eyes blinking at once.

"I don't like spiders." My voice shook. "Even the small ones freak me out. I once screamed when one crawled on my toe."

Ash didn't smile or laugh at me, but the bridge of his nose pinched, and he brought me closer to him. "Come, let me show you, they won't harm you."

With my heart racing, Ash led me toward the bridge. I pressed in closer to him because these monstrous spiders had me twitching with fear. He let go of my hand and wrapped an arm around my back, holding me closer.

The spider guards bowed their heads at our approach, making an eerie hissing sound.

I moved especially fast as we passed them and entered the golden bridge. My skin still crawled, and I needed another shower because I felt like insects were crawling all over me.

"You okay?" he asked.

I glanced back at the guards who held their post. "As long as they don't come near me, I'll be fine."

I breathed slightly easier the farther we moved from them, and we broke into a more normal stroll along the bridge that stretched toward another tower in the distance.

Towers and bridges surrounded us, some of the structures glinting iridescent where the sun touched. The lustrous rain-bow-like play of colors seemed so out of place in this hellish, dry world. Other towers were completely black and looked to be encased by a thin layer of web. I bet the spider creatures lived there, and that was where I would never visit. We approached an organic shaped building reminding me of a shrub, stems of steel poking outward.

Against the reddish sky, the vivid sunlight stretched out

with golden arms across the vertical city where everyone lived in towers.

Powerful heat came from both below and overhead. Even in my thin dress, I sweated.

Each time the hot wind blew past, the whole structure swayed slightly left and right, leaving me stumbling on my feet.

Ash held onto me though, and I figured if he wasn't freaking out, I had to be safe.

"What's a Gazen?" I asked, mostly to distract myself and understand what the monsters were talking about back at the table.

"A sand beast who hunts and feeds on anyone with a heart-beat," he answered bluntly.

I cut him a sharp look, my mouth partially open with a gasp. "And it lives in the city?"

He laughed softly, the sound so beautiful that it covered me in goosebumps. "They reside outside the walls. The city of Wyld is built on an enormous lava pit to make it impossible for them to reach us should they breach the walls."

"So the lava kills them. That's not such a bad thing."

"The problem is that they're trying to burrow through the walls, which will destabilize our towers and bridges. Every-thing's connected to the walls you see, perfectly balanced. And lately, the creepers have been trying to break down our walls and gates."

I swallowed past my dried throat, immediately distressed by the news. "And you all live with those things circling you like sharks?"

He shrugged nonchalantly. "The solution is to eliminate them. Creed is working on a plan. But most of the city popu-lation worries more about their next feed than stopping them. Now, come, let me show you your city."

Every cell in my body quivered at the fact that the

monsters were trapped in their home by more terrifying creatures.

I didn't say anything, but I suddenly felt less safe in Wyld, which said a lot considering I wasn't safe to begin with.

For what felt like hours, we walked from one bridge to another, learning that the towers were like apartment buildings where all the monsters lived, worked, and spent all their time. There were several fields in the city too, where they held regular hunting games. Something Ash said I would never view. It left me slightly terrified to find out what they hunted exactly.

Every monster we passed gave us a wide berth, bowing their respects at Ash. Most avoided looking at him at any cost, which I enjoyed as it meant they left me alone.

Some sported black holes for faces. Others looked more alien than human with multiple arms or legs. Then there were the shadow creatures who only slinked against hard surfaces. They creeped me out.

One stood plastered with its back to a dark wall. I might have missed it if it wasn't for the glint of its yellow eyes, looking right at me.

"Don't look so obvious. Monsters smell fear," Ash said. "Your hand twitches, and your breath picks up whenever we pass anyone."

"I'll try," I commented dryly. "So, you can hear them approaching?"

He smiled, and it was hard to ignore how perfectly striking he looked. Did he even realize how captivating he was? When he smiled, I had a hard time concentrating, because seeing his face only brought back memories of him in my dreams.

How he'd dote on me with such tenderness that after a hard day at the asylum, I sought out his gentle touches.

"Some creatures release energies I pick up on," he said. "Like the Umbre shadow critters. Their presence buzzes across my skin. But I pick up on yours as well. Like right now, your scent deepened slightly, just as it did in the dreams the more aroused you became." The corners of his mouth lifted.

He knew the impact he had on me, and judging by this smirk, he loved every second of it.

"Guess there's no hiding anything from you," I teased.

"You can try," he answered with a challenge, drawing me into a faster pace on feet that became more sore the longer we walked, and we hadn't even seen half the city yet.

We passed a group of monsters sitting at a table playing a board game, most of them appearing ragged, with broken scales across their skin. By the look of it, they'd decayed as if their bodies were preparing to break down. They were using eyeballs as pieces on the chequered board, and I bit down on my lip to not gasp aloud and draw attention to us.

Ash just laughed at me and drew me into a second tower nearby. The next thing I knew, we stepped into an elevator and were buzzing sideways. Everything left me disorientated, and yet when pressed in his arms, I felt a notch of comfort and safety with him.

Despite Ash's monstrous form back on the balcony being terrifying, he was like a huge cuddly bear, which had to be rare. I'd never met a man like him before.

"Where are we going?"

Ash moved to stand at my side, his hand on my lower back, shifting to my ass, and my breath hitched.

"A place I think you'll love. It's where I sometimes go to escape."

"Hopefully it's calmer than out there," I answered, his hand so hot, the heat crawled up my back.

"You're naked underneath your dress," he stated the obvious. "That's why your scent is stronger."

"Well, you see, Freddy was in charge of my new clothes, and that included no panties or shoes apparently."

Ash grumbled under his breath, a tension in his breathing. "He works hard but lacks knowledge of humans. Leave it with me, I'll fix this."

"Does it bother you that I'm not wearing any underwear?"

"Oh, Blake. You're like a little bird caught in the dangerous world of... Hmm. What are those flesh-eating birds you have on earth?"

"Vultures?"

"Yes, that's it. You are so innocent, not even aware of the danger lurking around you in our realm while vultures surround you. Many city dwellers may not see you as anything but food, and many will kill to fuck you if they lose themselves to your scent. That's why we must be careful."

My cheeks heated up and my stomach twisted in on itself. Tucking my chin into my chest, I took a quick whiff, smelling nothing but the shampoo I'd used in the shower. Were monsters able to smell that easily?

"Stop," Ash called out, bringing the elevator to a halting pause, and I stumbled to not fall over. Ash caught me, drawing me close and back to my feet.

His nostrils flared as he took another inhale, making a strange trilling sound I hadn't heard before from him.

"What was that?" I asked, still clutching onto his arms.

I sensed his trembling touch against me, and instantly, my alarm bells were going off. "Ash, are you okay?"

I heard him growl, the tension in his muscles shifting. "I've been trying really hard, little bird. Really hard to restrain myself. But you smell so fucking delicious. And it's so over-powering in here. I promised Creed I'd keep you safe." Yet he stood in front of me, his chest rising and falling faster, his nostrils expanding with each inhale.

"Maybe we just need to get out of the elevator," I suggested, alarmed at how easily my breathing grew erratic,

112

and in my mind, I pictured him fucking me up against this wall.

I squeezed my eyes tight to chase away the image, aware that the more I thought about it and clenched my thighs together, the wilder I'd drive Ash.

"Perhaps that's a good idea." Despite his words, he set a hand against the wall over my shoulder and leaned closer.

I stared into that familiar face from my dreams where I watched lust wash over his expression, where he lost himself and claimed me over and over in every possible position.

"I want you to be a good girl for me, to have you submit to me, to fill your mouth and pussy with my cock. Images of you spread for me spear through me, killing me," he admitted. "When you were lost to us for months, I was slowly going insane, craving your smell and taste, dying to sink into you."

Swallowing hard, I fought the arousal slithering through me. Just like the other men, Ash simply had to look at me a certain way, brush against me, and the nerve running across my pussy pulsed. Just as it was doing now.

"It's not helping to tease yourself this way," I said, my voice cracking. Or me.

His other hand stroked my cheek, then trailed down the length of my neck and paused on my shoulder.

A moan slid from my lips because he wasn't the only one struggling with emotions I only lost control of in my dreams. The beat of silence between us stretched out, and I did the only reasonable thing I could. I ducked out from under his arm and moved to the opposite side of the elevator, gasping for air.

"We should get going," I said.

Ash hadn't moved, and he scared me. Then he suddenly said, "Top floor." The raspy elevator voice repeated, *top floor.*

Ash pulled back, his shoulders straightening, and cracked his neck. He turned to me once more, the soft smile back on his face. "I hope I didn't frighten you. Sometimes, I struggle to hold back my monster."

I nodded. "It was just a bit dramatic, but I survived," I said with lightness in my voice, knowing that deep inside, he was a nice guy, incredibly handsome, and had a shameless addiction to sex.

The elevator doors slid open, and Ash reached his hand down to his pants, adjusting his bulge.

We emerged into a foyer made of white marble and immediately looked past the monsters in uniforms, wanting to hand us towels.

My sight was caught on the open doors leading outside to a paradise. Lush green trees, shrubs, and oversized flowers that reminded me of the monstrous, man-eating one from the Little Shop of Horrors. No sign of the desert, only the bright sky with a blushing red sun, and an oasis.

"What is that?" I gawked, smiling wildly and hoping we were going in there. I'd had enough of the scorching hot city.

Four monsters with spikes running down their backs knelt in front of Ash.

"What's going on?" I asked.

"They're showing me respect because this tower is run by Creed's circle," he murmured, and after he said something to them in a language I didn't understand, we headed into the lush paradise. I practically bounced on my toes.

Gone was the oppressive heat, the overwhelming chaos of towers and bridges, or monsters everywhere. There was silence, and I wanted to sink down and just take it all in.

I kept going, following the pebbled footpath that snaked amid the greenery. "I love this place already," I said, turning on the spot to look at Ash. Something glinted across his face, his breathing speeding up, his mouth curling into a dizzying smile.

"This haven was built to resemble the human forests," he

said. "There are no natural woodlands in the Shadowburn realm, so this was created as part of a study researching energies we can draw from human plants."

"So, this is the garden where everything is grown?"

"Yes, but not exactly."

"That makes no sense," I responded just as we emerged into a clearing surrounded by lofty fir trees, full of green leaves. My mouth dropped open at the lake, easily the size of half a football field ahead of us.

Crystal water glistened beneath the sun, small waves lapping at the edges from the breeze. The grass blades grew in greens, golds, and pinks.

I couldn't stop myself, but I ran forward, needing to touch the water and see if it was real. Everything I'd seen up to now was hot and dry.

Reaching the lake's edge, I kicked off my sandals and stepped into the shallow water on the bank.

Cool, crisp water ran between my toes, up to my ankles. And I laughed like a child. "This is incredible," I called back to Ash who strolled closer, with that sexy saunter, his hair wind-blown, and a smile that could easily make a girl forget she'd been kidnapped and taken to a monster realm. "I can't even believe this exists in the city."

"You can go for a swim," he offered, and I didn't even need to be told twice. Ripples danced across its clear surface, and the cool water ruffled around my legs, cooling me down.

I stepped deeper into the water, lifting my dress to my knees.

"You will need to strip," Ash told me, with a smile on his face. "It's illegal to swim with clothes in the lake."

I couldn't help but burst out laughing at him. "Now, I know you're making things up." It wasn't like he could see me naked anyway.

"If you break the rules, you'll force me to punish you."

"Right, of course you will." I realized he was wanting me to give him any excuse to claim me. So, I smirked and yanked my dress up and over my head, before tossing it over on the lawn. We were alone out here that I could see. "Well, problem solved." I turned to the water and dove into its crisp embrace.

The earlier heat danced from my body, and I grinned crazily under the water at how incredible it felt in here. If this tower was owned by Creed, then I'd be safe to come here as often as possible.

My head broke the surface, and I blinked and opened my eyes to the sight of Ash standing on the bank of the lake, studying me.

"It's so perfect. I might just stay here forever." I swam across the length of the water, away from Ash. When I glanced back, I couldn't ignore the bulge in his pants.

"You are spectacular how your tiny body glides through the water. I want to fuck your ass now," he admitted.

I huffed then laughed. Despite his abruptness, he had a way of improving my mood and making me feel sexy. "I don't think so."

I dove under and swam across the sandy bottom, thinking that maybe it wasn't all doom and gloom in this world.

When I came up for air, I found Ash talking to Freddy near the path, and that earlier unease surfaced. I could only imagine whatever they talked about, it would not be good news.

Moments later, he strode in my direction, carrying a towel in his hands. "I'm sorry, little bird. But I have to return you to our tower. Creed needs my help."

And just like that, my bright mood darkened, even as I still enjoyed the cool embrace of the water, which would be short-lived.

Chapter 9

Seven

Gazen blood leeched onto my hands.

Not much made me gag, but their filth was like acid. Leave it on your skin for too long, and it would start eating away at your flesh, down to your bones. I'd witnessed it firsthand. Sighing in frustration, I marched into the bathroom and scrubbed the shit off my hands.

What irritated me the most was that I'd been dragged away from Blake, and as a result, I'd been distracted in battle. Just as I had been the other day.

From the moment we'd heard Creed was bringing her to Wyld, I'd been beside myself to meet her in person. I'd spent nights with her over the past few years, everything about her imprinted on my mind...leaving me desperate. My body and cock craved her. Just thinking of her had me hardening as more memories sank me into the deluged chaos she caused in my head. A storm of desires and emotions I'd kept to myself for a long time.

And with her in Wyld, everything had changed, hadn't it?

The delicious pink-haired girl was with us now, permanently. And I'd have to deal with the rising feelings that worried me. I craved to offer her the world...but I was broken badly.

I growled at how easily she fell into my thoughts, so as quickly as I removed my jacket, I wrenched myself out of my memories, knowing I only tortured myself.

Pushing the sleeves of my shirt to my elbows, I studied the healed scars poking out from under the fabric like serpents slithering down my arms.

A shiver ran up my spine, a familiar darkness crawling over my skin.

With it came maniacal laughter that rang in my head, and *he* shifted under my skin.

"Fuck, no, not you," I growled under my breath. "Just go the fuck away."

I'd realized early on that something was *wrong* with me, but it had taken a few years to realize what it was. I had seven personalities, each more fucked up than the next. Or at least Creed referred to them as seven distinct personalities. Maybe he was right, or perhaps I preferred to keep all my emotions separated. I didn't know, in all honesty, except that some days it felt like I could barely keep my shit together, and those were the times that *he* came forward. The strongest of my voices. The most violent and depraved one of them all.

Silence swallowed me, and I gripped the edge of the sink, head low, shaking.

Darkness crept over me the more I looked at the scars on my arms, coming at me so fast I couldn't stop the past memories from shattering me...

The whip came down across my back like lightning.

I bellowed, the pain excruciating, my skin splitting. I growled with each strike, hating that I let them see my agony. Blood welled from under my sliced flesh, trailing down my body.

"You fucked up, didn't you?" my torturer growled. "She'd been ours, and you took her. For that, we'll take your life."

A frigid chill flooded me, and I wrenched my head up as my heart gave a jolt. I frantically tugged against the restraints that held my arms chained to the ceiling, my legs bound.

I blinked one good eye–the other was too puffy and sore to open.

Inhaling the bitter scent of my blood and perspiration, I stared into the impossible dark at my enemies.

Monsters who flitted around me, screeching for my death.

"She'll never be yours," I croaked. "Kill me, do your best, but every single one of you will starve."

That triggered them.

And maybe I wanted it to because my end was close... They came at me with claws and teeth. The whip licked around my neck with such ferocity that I choked out, "Kill me!"

Exhaling loudly, I shook away Seven and his depressing shit that clung to me. Fuck! It'd been too long since I made a show... too long for my liking. It was my turn to fix up the mess he constantly made.

I jerked my head up from the sink, looking at my reflection in the mirror. Violet eyes stared back, against a face hidden behind a damned mask over half my face. The hood threw shadows over my eyes.

Seven was a broken bastard, so lost to his torment that he hid in the dark and behind clothes.

Which was perfectly fine. That was where I came in.

I ripped the mask off my face, hating when he fucking wore it, and dropped it into the sink. There were no scars on his face for him to pity himself about. I drove the hood off my head too, the coolness refreshing. Light hair bounced wildly around my face, falling freely in jagged wisps.

I tilted my head back, a monstrous cry tearing free from my throat, and cracked my back. It had been too damn long since I had a chance to come out to play, to sharpen my teeth.

And I intended to make up for lost time. I whipped away

from the sink and marched out into the hallway, my sights set on going hunting down in the field. There were rules I tried to abide by, like no killing other monsters in Wyld unless they deserved it. Well, the 'deserved' part was open to interpretation.

Fiends who'd sinned were tossed into the field as sacrifices. They had been given one chance to escape the field–if they got out, then they were free. Unlucky bastards never made it out because once they entered, anyone who caught them could do as they pleased with them. So, it turned into a frenzied hunting match, everyone starving to spill blood.

And it had been too damn long since a hunt had been initiated. I had a craving to hack through sinew and bone with my bare teeth, to feel the warm trickle of blood sprayed on my face.

With a grunt, I pushed down the hallway, making my way to the elevator, intending to avoid Creed and the others. They only pissed me off when they got in my face, insisting on accompanying me. Something about not trusting me... Fuck that.

The hungry rush of my need filled my ears.

Something sweet suddenly filled my nostrils on my next inhale, and I paused, sucking in another intake of breath.

Sweetness coated the back of my throat, and my heart fluttered with excitement. Well, well. Maybe this would be a much better distraction after all.

I pivoted away from the elevator and took the hallway to my right, lengthening my steps, moving quickly through the maze of hallways. I turned a corner and there she stood.

The pretty human girl. A flower amid a field of weeds.

Long pink hair draped down her back, curved hips hugged by her black dress, and long legs made for being spread.

She was at the end of the hall in front of a potted plant,

plucking the leaves from a stem and stuffing them into her mouth.

I gagged. Humans could be such gross things, eating all sorts of crap. Had Creed been starving her to the point where she resorted to eating the decorations in our home?

I watched her pluck more leaves, leaving half the plant completely bare. She chewed on them hungrily, and even made tiny moaning sounds.

Desire. It drummed in my veins, and my cock hardened at the sight of her in a dress, hair brushed off her face, and her cheeks blushed. I strolled around the corner, drawing her attention.

She turned quickly, flustered at seeing me, tossing the few leaves in her hand back into the potted plant. "Seven. I didn't hear you." The faint hum of her voice was music to my ears.

Desperation bled through me to break her, to hear her scream, to remind her that she meant nothing to me. Seven had to get her out of his head because last time he listened to his heart, we ended up in a situation with me needing to intervene and deal with all his shit.

Strong, calculated steps brought me to her side. "You know, I can order you more salad if you're still hungry," I offered, eying her up and down, breathing in that intoxicating honeyed scent that lingered around her.

"Oh, you saw that." She glanced at the half-stripped plant, then back at me, her cheeks blushing brighter. "I know it looks bad, but one of the servers in the tower told me these leaves were edible and put the plant here in case I wanted a snack. Of course, I thought they were crazy, but then," she shrugged a shoulder, "I decided to give it a try. And you wouldn't believe it. It tastes like chocolate. The dark, velvety kind that's my favorite. I have no idea what this plant is, but I need a whole forest of them. Imagine eating chocolate-flavored salad. I'd never gain any weight."

She rambled, and I didn't understand half of what she was saying. "So, you're out here all alone?"

"I'm not far from my room." She pointed to the door several feet away with her chin before facing me again, her gaze darting all over my features. "I kind of like this look on you with no mask or hood." She batted her eyes, and something inside me tightened, my body drawn to every inch of her.

The longer I stared at her, the more fire scorched my insides.

Seven's longing and agony balled up in my gut, and a wild growl rumbled in my chest. Because if he didn't have the balls to do it, then I'd remind this human girl why Seven wasn't interested in her.

Then he'd get his shit together and not give a fuck what anyone thought of how he looked. Let alone her...

"You need to return to your room," I said, giving her an out. No one could say I was a fucking bastard.

"And if I don't?" Tenacious and stupid, she met my gaze with her challenge.

I grinned slowly at her response. "Then I'll remind you why you're not safe here... even with us."

Her lips pinched, arms stiffened by her side. "I see you're in *that* mood."

Something about her tone of voice, or maybe it was the patronizing words, but before I knew it, I had her by an arm and was hauling her into her room.

She dragged her feet, fighting me. I'd admit, there was something mesmerizing about a little thing like her thinking she stood any chance against me.

I was starved of real fear, of feeding. I had her pressed up against the floor to ceiling window in no time, her face to the glass, my groin against her ass.

"Get off me," she snarled.

"That's not what you really want, is it?" I purred in her

ear. "You want to be fucked. That's why you're acting up, aren't you, my little brat?"

Lust licked over my cock, the primal need within me not what I expected. I blamed it on Seven corrupting our body with the constant need to feed on her. My cock thickened painfully.

She shuddered as I ground my erection against her.

Being attracted to her was a rarity for me since I hungered for blood, war, and suffering. Yet heat raged inside me. Her body wriggled against mine for escape, which only made me harder.

Caging her body with mine, I stilled my mind, closed my eyes for a few moments to ground myself. To not let this small human distract me.

"What do you want? To feed?" she asked with nervous amusement.

Opening my eyes, I murmured, "To remind you of your place."

She twisted her head to look at me, flashing me those silvery eyes and the terror behind them. "I'm not afraid of you," she stated, yet she trembled when I reached for her throat, closing my claws around her frail neck.

With my other hand, I tore her dress off in one savage move, leaving her completely naked and pressed to the window for anyone to see.

She gasped, shaking violently now. I reveled in the sound, her naked flesh burning against my body.

"Are you afraid now?"

"Fuck you," she snapped, and I loved the fire in her voice.

"See out there," I stated, forcing her to look outside. "Everything out there wants to kill you. Everything in the city wants to fuck you. You really are in a hard place, aren't you?"

"And where do you lay in that equation?"

I clicked my tongue, pressing my face into the softness of

her hair, inhaling the sweet, seductive smell. My lips parted, teeth sharpening. How easy would it be to tear into her neck, to steal her breath away...

Don't kill, you asshole.

Fuck Seven and the memories of him constantly drumming shit into my head. I got it... The human was our savior and yet, all I craved was to hold her beating heart in my hand. Guess I'd have to take the next best thing... her ripe, juicy pussy.

"I'm still deciding," I whispered in her ear, my hand sliding down the curves of her body, skin silky under my touch and rippling with goosebumps. I easily understood why the others inside my head craved this morsel. She was spectacular.

"So, what's your story?" she asked, full of bravery, though her body quivered as I nudged her feet to spread her legs for me, pushing my knee between them.

"I have no story," I growled. "But you will after today. Now spread your legs wider for me like a dirty little girl."

She clenched her legs tighter instead against my bent knee pinned between hers. But no matter how much she fought, it was too late for her. Maybe for me too... that heady scent of sex flooded my nostrils, and I tasted it on my tongue, fogging my brain.

"You're an asshole, you know that," she snarled.

I tsked. "Stop squirming now."

"And you can go fuck yourself. Let me go."

I laughed, my clawed hand running down the length of her spine, and that perfect white flesh, leaving her gasping. Her gorgeous ass left me grabbing it, squeezing hard. With a single thought, my claws morphed into fingers because Creed would butcher me if I ruined Blake too much. Then I trailed bland, boring fingers between her legs.

She tensed, pushing against me, and I laughed. "Don't bother."

Her hitched breath turned me on ridiculously, my heart beating viciously. My fingers slid over the seam of her dripping wet pussy.

She tensed against me, her breaths racing.

"How does this feel?"

I parted her swollen lips. Despite the protesting moan on her throat, I pinched her clit with two fingers.

She writhed against me. "Like hell."

I chuckled. "I'll give you Hell if that's what you desire." Her captivating scent of sex drove me crazy. I needed to feel her jerking and crying out in my arms as she came.

"I hate you." Her voice trembled, while her scent pushed and pushed me, my dick twitching with the urgency to plunge into her, to fuck her so hard she'd never forget me.

"Good," I rasped in her ear. "Hate me while I make you cum, and I feed." Her scent bombarded my senses, and I pinched her clit a bit harder, her legs shuddering against me, the tortured groan on her throat a beautiful sound.

I couldn't help myself... I was sadistic like that. But I loved to hear the conflicted arousal in her voice. Releasing her, I unceremoniously buried two fingers into her tight cunt, her half cry, half moan sending delicious shivers down my back. She was so perfect, so ripe for the taking, so wet, and she wanted me despite her body shoving against mine.

Sucking down on my fingers, I felt her squeeze each time I fingered her, inflicting the punishment she craved.

I was lost to the lust she awoke in me, watching every twitch, every movement she made, knowing she fell closer to the edge of her orgasm. The agonizing ache in my balls to cum in her burned me up.

To say I was of two minds was an understatement. What to do with such a gorgeous girl with a soaking pussy sucking down on my fingers?

Fuck her.

Leave her wanting, begging me for more.

I almost laughed at myself at the thought as it was clear I couldn't walk away until I fucked her pussy. Until she exploded all over my cock.

She pressed her hands flush to the window, her tiny body shivering with wanton desires. When she didn't respond, I grabbed her hair and tugged her head back hard, her cries filling the room. It made my cock throb.

"Nothing in this world is what it seems, my flower. And definitely not me, so don't get your hopes too high."

"I know exactly who I'm dealing with," she groaned, her body quivering from how hard I fingered her. "And I don't fall in love with monsters..." Her words morphed into a scream.

"Oh, you're fooling yourself if you believe you'll find love here. We're all twisted assholes, too broken to feel such an emotion. But sex... well, that we'll revel in and take it from you over and over." I growled at how good she felt. "You're so tight. I can't wait for you to strangle my cock."

Her cries were beautiful, filling my ears, turning into a scream of beauty. Her pussy suddenly clenched hard down my fingers as she broke under the weight of her orgasm. The horny little bitch needed this, didn't she?

Writhing, she was spectacular, her body jerking, and I allowed her the time to enjoy the release as I kept rubbing her clit with my free fingers.

Heat filled every inch of me, and I gulped down the meal she offered me, knowing this was but a sampler of what was coming.

"Good girl. Scream for me. Suck on my fingers with that perfect little cunt."

She was fucking stunning, arching her back as she came undone all over my hand.

I studied every inch of her body's reaction, every tiny

moan she made. When she finally quieted down, gasping for air, I whispered, "How do you feel, Blake?"

The response never came and she remained pressed up against the window, making soft sounds.

I drew my fingers out of her sweet hole, and she released a sharp cry as I kept her pinned between me and the window, sticking my fingers into my mouth, licking them clean. Her muskiness swallowed me, and I shivered at how incredible she tasted on my tongue.

"Get off me," she croaked.

"I'm not even close to finishing with you." I spun her around by her shoulders to face me because I wanted to look into her eyes when I fucked her.

But she fell to her knees as though they gave out on her, her expression painted with such beautiful pain.

A tear rolled down her cheek, followed by a soft sob while fury burned behind her striking eyes.

And without hesitation, something came over me, something that felt like guilt.

No, that couldn't be me.

Something heavy scraped across my mind, wrenching me away from her. As quickly as I tried to hold onto the image of my small flower, darkness gathered over my thoughts, stealing me away.

You bastard, Seven...not fucking now.

And just like that, my world blacked out.

I snapped my head up, the blur of the room and *him* vanishing came quickly. I stumbled back, blinking at the sight of Blake in front of me, her aroused scent engulfing me.

A hand on her stomach, the other rubbing away the tears, her shoulders curled forward like a wounded animal.

So fragile. So innocent.

Devastation tore through my soul. The sight of her savaged my heart, knocking the wind out of me.

My insides carved in half with what *he'd* done, my chest splintering.

"Blake," I whimpered, flinching when she reared away from me. That single movement ripped me to shreds, and I backed away, knowing the damage was done. "I'm so fucking sorry."

I couldn't bear the way she glared at me with hatred. Shuddering, I twisted away from her side and stormed out of her room knowing that *he'd* really fucked me up this time.

Chapter 10

Blake

"I love you. I don't know why I never said that," murmured Steele as he leaned in and brushed his lips against mine. Sparks erupted in my insides. He loved me? And...he'd just kissed me?

It was official. I'd died and gone to heaven.

"I'm coming to get you. I'm so sorry I let this happen."

"Come get me?" I murmured, my mind spinning with the words that had just come out of his mouth. I looked around the room, trying to get my bearings. I was still in my bedroom in the tower, but everything had a hazy aura to it, like a soft fog was floating through the air.

Before I could think any closer about what he was saying, his lips touched mine again. The kiss remained soft, and he pulled back to stare into my eyes, his surreal, ice blue eyes holding me captive.

He must have seen the longing in my gaze because his next kiss was deeper...demanding. His tongue slid into my mouth, and I could taste his hunger for me.

I had spent hours upon hours thinking of what his kiss

would be like when it happened. But this...this was a million times better than I could have ever imagined.

I was dripping wet. Instantly.

Those hands that I'd stared at during my sessions with him ——a bit creeper-like, I'd admit——began to move over my hips and thighs, squeezing as he went along. I moaned when they slid to my ass and he cupped my cheeks.

"Fuck. You are fucking perfect. An angel sent to torture me," he growled as his hands slid under the gauzy nightgown I'd changed into before going to bed, and began to slide it up my skin.

There was something trying to slide into my consciousness, but I couldn't quite grasp it. And as his hands smoothed along my legs, and then up my thighs, and then to my hips, all thoughts flew away.

He moaned when my underwear came into view, the sexiest fucking moan I'd ever heard. I watched as his pupils dilated and his nostrils flared as he stared transfixed at the wet spot on my panties that I knew was there.

"You are the sexiest fucking thing I've ever seen," he purred, and I flushed under his praise, wanting more of it. As much as I could get.

He gently laid me down, and I shivered, just anticipating where this was going. Steele leaned between my legs and softly bit one of my inner thighs, and then the other. I tensed as he paused for a long moment before burying his face in my underwear and taking a long inhale.

"Fuck," he purred, and a soft gasp escaped my throat.

He abruptly pulled away and then he grasped the fabric of my nightgown and tore it open.

"I thought I had time. I thought I could tell you how much you were my whole fucking world," he said in a hitched voice as his gaze ran up and down my body in awe. "I'm never going to fuck us up again."

His hands gripped onto my hips and he pulled me into his lap, his hard length sliding in between my legs and nestling right between my folds so perfectly it was like he'd been made for me. My head fell back as he began to slowly grind me against his length...his huge length. Once he'd got the rhythm going and my hips were moving in sync with him, one of his hands left my hip and gripped my hair in his fist so he could lift my head up so that I was looking at him again. He thrust against me, his pants, and my underwear, not doing anything to stop the surge of pleasure coursing through my body every time we moved against each other.

Steele was biting his bottom lip, and I could have come from the sight alone, even if he wasn't hitting my clit perfectly. He pulled my hair gently and angled me backwards so that my bare breasts were thrust forward like an offering. He growled as his lips descended on first one nipple, and then the other, the warm heat of his mouth lapping at my tips until I found myself practically sobbing and pulling on his hair as I held him against me.

"Dreamed about these fucking tits." *He gave each one a rough suck before moving back to my mouth.* *"You're soaking my pants, sweetheart,"* *Steele murmured as one of his hands moved between our bodies and he began to lightly rub circles on my clit through my soaking wet panties.*

"Please," *I gasped, and he laughed in a sexy, raspy tone that was enough to send me flying over the edge, my orgasm wracking through me until I was a sobbing, writhing mess...who couldn't wait to have more.*

"Yes. Fuck. Nothing sexier. Nothing better than the sweet sounds of you coming," *he growled as he shifted me off him and then practically ripped his pants off in his urgency to get back to me.*

He claimed my lips desperately as he grabbed my underwear and tore it off. My attention was on his dick though.

Was it...ridged and gray? I blinked and it was back to a

regular human dick, albeit a huge one that was beyond perfect, just like him.

Steele aggressively lifted me up and pulled my knees apart until I was stretched over him.

"Tell me you want this," he ordered, and all I could do was whimper in response.

Without another word, he slammed me down on top of him, spearing me on his length that was so long I could've sworn he was nudging at my cervix.

He held me still for a long moment, his face almost pained-looking.

"Steele?" I asked desperately, needing him to move before I lost my mind. When he opened his eyes though, I gasped when I looked into eyes that had been completely overtaken by glowing ice blue, no sign of the white or black of his pupils. He blinked again, and his eyes were back to normal.

That sensation that I needed to pay attention to something came roaring back. My mind was having trouble under-standing what was going on, though. It felt like I was hallu-cinating.

"You're so fucking wet," he whispered, his lips brushing against mine.

He abruptly lifted me up and then thrust up into me again. His thrusts began to move faster, and I threw my arms around his neck, sounds coming out of my mouth that were almost inhuman.

"This is perfect. You're perfect," he moaned. When I began to move up and down in a rocking motion on his dick, his hands moved to my breasts, gently kneading and tugging at my nipples. I began to ride him harder, loving how perfectly full I felt. I still couldn't believe this was happening with him.

Something pounded against my brain once again, but then he made a delicious needy noise and I was right back in the moment. He kissed and licked at my lips, our breaths melding *together. Everything was a sensory overload—the sound of our skin slapping together, his intoxicating smell, the little moans coming out of both of us.*

"I. Fucking. Love you," he growled, and happiness like I'd never thought I'd experience washed against my skin.

But then something began to happen. Right before my eyes, wisps of black smoke wrapped around us and the icy blue of his eyes completely took over the white and black again. The inky black mist softly brushed against my skin as Steele changed forms. His already perfect muscles became somehow even more defined and his tan skin changed into a dark gray color. It was like his whole body had become wrapped in the smokey-colored mist. I cried out as an orgasm hit me just then, his appearance and the beyond pleasurable sensations coursing through my body leaving me completely disoriented.

"Steele, what's happening?" I gasped, but when I blinked again, he was back to normal. It said a lot for how caught up in the moment I was that I continued to bounce on top of him—either that, or I'd just had enough experience with otherworldly creatures I was turned on even more by the sight at this point. His cock was stretching me wide open as his form began to flicker back and forth between the black mist covered gray creature and his familiar, regular form.

"I'm coming to find you, sweetheart," he murmured, seeming to be completely unaware of what I was seeing.

Abruptly the tendrils of mist wrapped around me, preventing me from moving at all somehow.

"My turn," he muttered against my skin as he began to thrust up into me and work every pleasure spot on my body.

"Don't stop," I begged, as his form stopped changing, leaving me with his beautiful, dark gray form in front of me.

"You're sucking my cock. Such a greedy pussy. So freaking tight. You're such a good girl," he growled, and I flushed again under his praise. "Letting me fuck you so good. You're so fucking

hot," he breathed as his fingers pinched my nipples and I was held perfectly in place by the mist enveloping both of us.

"You're milking my cock, sweetheart. Such a fucking good girl."

His words...and everything else he was doing, did it for me, and I screamed as the most powerful orgasm I'd ever experienced crashed through my body. Almost simultaneously, I felt the heat of him inside me filling me up to the point I was overflowing with his cum, and it dripped back out and down my thighs and his dick.

He thrust a few more times before he slowed and finally leaned his forehead against mine.

"I'm coming to get you, Blake. Wait for me," he whispered.

And then he was gone.

I sat up with a gasp, my chest heaving as I came out of my dream. Frantically, I searched the shadows of my room, a part of me sure that he would be there.

Steele's glowing blue eyes haunted my mind. The mist. The dark gray tint of his skin. The way he'd grown. I'd just imagined that, right? My sick desire for monsters from years of being programmed by Creed and the others in my dreams had combined with my desire for Steele. That's all it was. I grabbed at my nightgown, noting that I was still fully dressed.

My skin was slicked with sweat and my hair was stuck to the back of my neck.

And I was throbbing between my legs.

Just like all my dreams with the monsters, it had seemed so real.

But I didn't know how to wrap my mind around the idea of Steele...being one of them.

A breeze brushed over my skin, and I shivered, frowning when I saw that the window to my room was open. How had it gotten open? I looked around my room again, half expecting something to be hiding in the shadowed corners, but there was no one there.

It was dark outside, but the dark here was a dark burning red color that looked completely different than what I was used to.

Who was I kidding? Everything looked completely different than what I was used to. I'd eaten leaves off of a random plant. I had regular interactions with a gelatinous slug-looking creature with shark-like teeth. The guards were spider monsters.

The sex dreams with monstrous creatures was about the only thing the same as my old life. A hysterical laugh slipped from my lips and I took a deep breath, trying to get ahold of myself.

I slipped out of bed and walked slowly to the slightly open window to look out down below at the city now in view if you stuck your head out. I wasn't surprised at all to see that the city looked far livelier than it had before. Why wouldn't the monsters come out more at night? Did they even sleep? I mean, the scary stories of monsters coming out at night had to have a basis somewhere, right? And the particular group of monsters in my life had certainly been all about the night.

I made a mental note to ask one of them something about that later. A loud cry from one of the bridges down below sounded, and I leaned over further out the window to see what was going on. There was a swarm of them gathered on one of the bridges. And they appeared to be...dancing? Maybe that was a thing.

A dinosaur-looking creature suddenly flew in front of my window, its flapping wings snapping through the air and shaking the windowsill and glass. It hovered inches away from me, and I stumbled back, a scream caught in my throat as I stared wide-eyed at the creature, expecting it to dart through the opening.

I inched my way back to the window and struggled to close it, keeping my eyes out for any flying creatures.

But I couldn't get the window to move at all.

I did not want to be alone in this room right now. Biting my lip, I glanced at the door, wondering if any of my monsters would be out and about.

My monsters. Every time I thought about that, I considered having a lobotomy. Especially after what Seven...or one of Seven's demons, had done to me.

Except you liked it.

I tried to ignore that thought, but then of course Steele's image had to fill my mind once again. And when I looked over at the bed and saw the winged beast glaring menacingly at me from the wall, I decided to chance it and leave my room to see if Ash or Creed were out there. My need for distraction, and closed windows, outweighed everything else at the moment.

I opened the door and then peered out into the hallway. The lighting was muted, but it didn't give creepy haunted house vibes. So I guess that was a plus. The reddish light of the night fell through the glass dome ceiling of the hallway, bathing everything in red.

And it was so quiet.

I walked down the hall in the direction I thought I'd been before, not seeing anyone. I turned left and saw that the windows that lined this hallway were all open and a gentle breeze was blowing through the openings.

I began to creep down the hallway, my head swiveling like a crazy person as I tried to look for the creatures. One of them zoomed by the open window, and this time I did fully scream.

A dark chuckle came from behind me and I swirled around, my heart pounding in my chest.

It was Tempest, surprisingly not in his monster form. Which was a good thing because I didn't think I could take that kind of scare on top of the flying bird/dinosaur monsters flapping around.

I'd never been alone with him, not in my dreams, nor at any point since coming here. I shifted uneasily, uncomfortable with it happening right now.

"Not a fan of the Avis?" he chuckled again, walking slowly towards me, like how a predator stalked his prey. Even though I knew I shouldn't, I found myself taking a step backwards, regretting my decision to leave my room if this was who I was going to end up with.

Tempest was beyond hot, and sex with him had been... incredible. But out of all of them, he was the most selfish one. It felt like he was taking something from me every time we touched.

"My first interaction with them was watching a bird grab one of you and fly away," I responded stiffly, trying to keep the fear out of my voice as he continued to walk towards me.

"They do have a habit of doing that," he commented, his emerald eyes boring into me and seeming to glow in the dim lighting. As he walked, he began to change, his eyes shifting into dark slits, his body growing until he was at least three feet taller than his other form, and his razor-sharp teeth and horns emerging. His body lengthened into shadows, parts of him extending into the corridor behind him.

I bit the side of my cheek in an effort not to cry out. "The Avis are nothing compared to the creatures that stalk the palace, Blake," he purred, his voice sounding like a hiss as he fully morphed into his monster.

Unlike with the others, where the lust and fear I felt whenever I saw them in their monster forms went hand in hand—all I was feeling right now was fear.

Another Avis flew by, and this time I didn't even flinch. All of my attention was centered on Tempest.

I'd taken one more step and then stood my ground,

hoping a show of strength would get him to stop whatever power trip he was on right now.

Unfortunately, it did nothing.

"Fear and arousal—my favorite combination," he said as he finally got to within a few inches of me, his form towering over mine. A long tongue slid out of his fanged, smiling mouth. I guessed he was smiling. The whole skeletal look he had going made it hard to tell. His tongue grazed my cheek, and it took everything in me not to flinch. A rattling sound came from his chest, a macabre soundtrack that sent my heart racing.

His slitted nostrils expanded, and if I could have seen his eyes clearly, I was sure that they would have been rolled back in ecstasy.

"I think I'll go back to my room right now," I murmured as his tongue began to wrap around my neck.

"I haven't had a chance to play with you, little Blake. You're not trying to leave me out now, are you?"

His tongue tightened around my neck, and I gasped as it started to become a struggle to breathe.

"We've never tried asphyxiation in our play, have we?" he asked silkily. "Now seems as good a time as any."

I stood there and stared into his slitted-snake-like eyes as his tongue continued to clench and my vision darkened around the edges. I started to creep towards unconsciousness —the last thing I would want in this situation.

I reached up and grabbed at his rope-like tongue, but it was much stiffer and harder than I'd assumed, and it felt like I was pulling at an iron necklace. I opened my mouth to scream for help, but all that came out was a gasp as the last of my oxygen slipped away.

"Tempest!" Creed's voice rocked through the hallway and Tempest's tongue immediately loosened and slid off of me... right before I was about to succumb and pass out. My hands wrapped around my throat and I stumbled backwards, gasping for breath as Creed came into view, his red eyes boiling over in rage.

Tempest stepped to the side and leaned against one of the pillars in between the windows nonchalantly, as if he hadn't just been choking me.

Creed shot him a glare as his tail wrapped around my waist and held me up, right before I was about to collapse.

My breath continued to come out in shocked gasps as the world spun around me. Creed's teeth and claws lengthened as he stared at Tempest.

"What the fuck were you doing?" Creed growled.

Tempest yawned like Creed had just asked about the weather. "Just a little playtime. You aren't the only one who gets to have some fun. You did say she was ours, did you not?" he challenged.

I scoffed. I'd learned from my dreams I was into some kinky shit. But that...that hadn't been meant to be kinky or sexy, or anything fun. That had been terrifying.

Creed picked me up with his tail and softly set me against the wall so that I would have something to lean against before unwrapping it from around me and stalking towards Tempest.

Tempest's eyes gleamed as he watched him, the darkness that surrounded him increasing in size to try and match Creed's large form.

"Let me be clear—if I ever see anything like that again, you will be cast out," Creed said in a dangerously smooth voice.

Tempest's gaze widened in surprise...and then anger. "So, it's like that then, brother?"

"It's exactly like that," replied Creed before reaching out and grasping onto one of Tempest's horns, and cracking it into pieces.

Creed turned his back and stalked towards me, not giving Tempest another look as his cries of pain echoed around us.

"Come here, pet," Creed crooned as he scooped me up from where I'd plastered myself to the wall and cradled me in his arms as we walked in the opposite direction from Tempest.

"You broke his horn," I whispered, staring in shocked awe as I watched Tempest over Creed's shoulder. Tempest's clawed fingers were fisted up and his whole body shook. He growled terrifyingly before stalking in the opposite direction from us.

"It will grow back. Tempest...just needs to be put in his place sometimes. He's complicated. He means no harm," said Creed calmly. Creed's claws softly stroked through my hair as he held me, and it was all I could do not to fucking purr at how good it felt. My whole body was relaxing despite the trauma I'd just gone through and the fact I wasn't so sure that Tempest didn't mean me harm.

We got to the threshold of a room I hadn't been in before, and I quickly realized that this must be Creed's private chambers. The entire far wall was made of glass and looked out on the city beyond it. There was a large platform bed with black silky sheets in the very middle of the room, and the stone walls were a moody, obsidian color.

"I guess this answers my question if monsters actually sleep," I murmured, as he strode towards the bed and set me down gently on the soft mattress.

"Very rarely, my pet," he answered as he continued to stroke through my hair, a soft growl emanating from his chest and lulling me to sleep like a comforting lullaby.

"I think we should mark choking off my list of sex things," I said drowsily as I slowly drifted into dreamland.

Creed's sexy, low laugh followed me into a deep sleep.

Chapter 11

Ash

"**F**uckity, fuck, fuck, fuck," I growled as the alarm rang out just as I'd gotten to the threshold of my home. *You've got to be fucking kidding me.* It had been constant the last few days, with more attacks on the walls than ever before.

But the alarm wasn't good. The alarm meant that one of the fuckers had made it in somehow—which was almost impossible considering the lava our city sat on. Which meant that someone had let something through the gates.

A headache pulsed in my skull as Creed stalked out of the entryway, looking ready to burn down the whole world. The asshole had somehow gotten to lay down next to Blake last night. I'd be ready to kill if I was dragged from that as well. As it was, I was ready to destroy everything that was keeping me working nonstop instead of being with her.

Had she been eating? Did she like the clothes in her room? Was she happy? I didn't know the answers to any of that right now, and it was literally eating away at me.

My twin appeared next, looking like even more of a sorry bastard than usual. He'd stared resolutely at the ground like it held the keys to the universe, his mask secured on his face and his hood draped over him. I shook my head and sighed, waiting for the fourth member of our little group to come out.

For a second my thoughts drifted to when there'd been five of us, but I quickly dashed those thoughts into pieces. I'd vowed never to spend a second thinking about that traitorous asshole again.

Tempest emerged in the doorway a moment later, looking annoyed at life. We all seemed to be in high spirits today.

"Report," Creed barked at Tempest, much more surly and short than usual.

Tempest gritted his razor-sharp teeth but refrained from snapping back at him. "Three Gazen. Someone let them through the far west gate."

Creed's eyes burned red and, fuck, the look on his face, it actually scared me. "Seven...when we're done dealing with this, see what you can find out," he said dangerously.

Seven, our resident spy of the group, nodded in response, and this time I really did roll my eyes. He was so fucking dramatic about everything.

"Let's go," Creed ordered, and I let out a loud war cry that had all of them looking at me like I'd gone crazy.

"Too much?" I asked, just eager to get this thing fucking over with so I could hang out with Blake.

I was hungry.

We set off on a steady run through the bridges. The city had slowed to a crawl, everyone hiding once they'd heard the alarms. The monsters in this city were fierce enough, but no one wanted to fight a Gazen if they didn't have to.

And besides, that's what they had us for.

It was still taking too long, and the closer we got, the more we could hear the destruction the creatures were wreaking in our city. Finally, Creed got frustrated with our slow journey; he took his knife from around his waist, and just as an Avis flew by, he jumped off the fucking bridge and grabbed onto one of its legs, its squawks and roars of rage filling the air. Creed dangled in the air while he pressed his knife into its soft stomach as it moved in the direction he wanted.

I groaned. I hated air travel.

But whatever would get me closer to Blake. I pulled out my own knife, and as another Avis flew by...I jumped.

Seven

Shame. It was all I could feel at the moment. I'd thrown myself into hunting the Gazen after what had happened with Blake...but nothing had been enough of a distraction to erase the memory of her face as she'd slid to the floor.

Blake's agony just hit different. It was all-encompassing.

With *her*...it had been different. I'd never been moved by the sight of our queen's moods. The only time I'd really felt something was after I'd been tortured...and she'd seen the aftermath of what they'd done to me, the scars that would never heal.

And she'd laughed in disgust and sent me out of her bedroom.

But even then, the disgust I'd felt...it hadn't compared to what had flashed through me when I saw that look in Blake's eyes.

Even when the queen died, I hadn't—

What the fuck was wrong with me? Having this much... feeling. For a human girl.

She's not just a human, something growled inside of me, and I took a deep breath. This wasn't the time for one of the others to come out and take over right now.

Roars filled my ears as we got closer to the Gazen. I pulled on the Avis to get it closer to the bridge below me so I could jump down. I hit the ground and growled as the Avis swiped at me with a wing, knocking me back a step. Tempest chuckled nearby and I gave him a middle finger, one of the few things from the human world that I enjoyed.

"You focused? Because I kind of like having you around," Ash joked quietly from beside me, and I nodded, not turning to look at him. My twin always seemed to know everything I was feeling. It was like he had a pathway into my soul.

Fucking annoying.

A scream tore through the air, and Creed took off at a sprint around the building we'd landed behind. The rest of us followed and—I smelled them before I saw them. I held in my vomit at the stench, the smell was always worse when they traveled in packs like this.

"Watch out!" Ash roared from behind me, and I jumped to the left as a Gazen barreled towards me. Fuck. He was a large motherfucker.

I shifted uneasily when I saw that somehow the three Gazen had ended up circling around us...almost like they had planned a trap.

That would be new...

A snarl ripped through my ears as Tempest was scooped up by one of them, the long tail circling around him in a vice grip. He struggled to free his arms, but the Gazen was coiled too tight. I ran at the beast, my knife held high, and I sliced down its side. It hissed in pain, but only coiled tighter.

Tempest was beginning to turn gray as the life was squeezed out of him, and my heart began to beat faster.

I flipped backwards as another of the creature's tails sliced down right where I'd been. That would have hurt.

Drops of the creature's blood rained down on my skin, sizzling as it fell from where Ash had just cut a long line down its stomach. My sleeve had pulled up from my efforts, so the blood had fallen right on one of my scars, suddenly flooding

144

me with memories of how I'd gotten the scar in the first place.

"What happened to you? You're hideous," she gasped in disgust as I lifted up my shirt, gritting my teeth at the pain. I needed her to heal me. That was the only way these cuts would go away.

"My queen," I murmured, reaching out to her.

She backed away. "You were perfect. Now—you're ruined."

I laughed weakly, ignoring the shame battering in my gut. The shame and confusion. I'd gotten these while protecting her. Why was she acting like this? "You know the cuts will fade with your touch. What's wrong with you?"

"I won't be fucking you tonight," she abruptly announced.

"Darling," Ash murmured, casting her a wary glance. "He needs you to—"

"I am queen. I don't need to do anything," she all but screeched. "Now get out," she ordered, casting me a disdainful glance.

I stared at her in shocked horror. If she didn't heal me, I was going to carry these scars forever.

"Seven! Watch out," I heard Creed cry from nearby, dragging me out of whatever mind fuck I'd just experienced to the clusterfuck going on around me. Before I could move, though, a fang tore through my back, popping out in front of me.

I choked as I stared at the fang in horror. Suddenly, the fang was ripped out of me and I toppled to the ground, hitting with a thud. Metallic blood flooded my mouth. Shit. That wasn't a good sign.

Fuck. I may actually die from this one.

I heard yells and screams around me, but they were all muffled, like I was underwater. I stared up at the red sky above me as cold began to creep into my veins.

And right before everything turned black, I saw her face. Blake's.

I'd never get to see her again.

BLAKE

"Blake," I heard Ash scream from somewhere in the castle. I darted towards my door and threw it open, not liking the pure terror in his voice.

"I'm here!" I called out, running towards the sound of his voice as he continued to try and call for me.

I turned a corner and saw him barreling up the stairs, a lifeless and pale-looking Seven thrown over his shoulder.

He stumbled in relief when he saw me. "Please, you have to help him," he cried. I nodded, shocked at what I was seeing.

There was a room to the left of us, and Ash threw open the door, darting inside. I ran in after them.

Ash laid Seven down gently on the bed that sat against the far wall, pulling at his hair in distress as he stared down at him.

"What can I do?" I asked, tears falling down my face when I saw the huge, ragged hole in the middle of his chest. I could see the blood spreading underneath him as he bled out.

Was this it? Was he just going to die?

I couldn't bear the thought.

Ash turned to me, desperation bleeding from his haunted gaze. "Please. Please help my brother."

"I—what do I do?"

"You have to let him feed off you. You have to have sex with him. Or something. Please!"

Ash wasn't really making sense, but I was distracted when Seven moaned suddenly and his eyes opened.

"Don't bother," he croaked. "I'm not worth it."

"Well, that's certainly not true," I murmured, my fingers already undoing the buttons on the front of the black silk dress I was wearing.

Seven's eyes were watching me hopelessly, his pallor drained of all vitality. I slipped the dress from my shoulders, and his eyes widened as he watched me.

"You're fucking perfect, princess," Ash murmured from behind me as his breath caressed my neck. "My brother is so fucking lucky." His hands made quick work of yanking off my bra and slipping my underwear down my hips. His touch sent shivers cascading down my skin.

"I'm thinking he might disagree with you on that one. The hole in his chest would say otherwise," I responded as I walked towards the bed.

"Blake," Seven choked out as I moved onto the bed ungracefully until I was straddling his legs. My fingers were trembling as I unbuttoned the top of the thick leather pants he was wearing, struggling a little as I slowly began to pull them down. He was so big and heavy, and he wasn't helping at all.

"I've got you, princess," Ash said as helped get his twin's pants down and then ripped Seven's shirt open, revealing his chiseled, scar-ridden chest.

That was kind of hot. I mean, it would be a lot hotter without the whole bleeding and gaping wound thing—but yeah...still hot.

Ash moved off the bed, but I was only faintly aware of him; all my attention was centered on the Adonis in front of me. His pants had been pulled down to his mid-thigh, and his long, thick cock was displayed.

"Oh fuck. Look at him, he's already improving just from the scent of your arousal filling the room," Ash purred. I reluctantly tore my eyes off his dick and looked up at his face. Oh. His color really did look like it was already getting better.

"Touch yourself, princess," Ash ordered. "Fill the room with the scent of your perfect dripping cunt."

My pussy gushed at his words.

"You like that," Ash growled, his voice growing deep and husky. "Fuck, you smell so good."

Ash's voice may have been a sexy soundtrack to the moment, but all my attention was focused on Seven, whose color was continuing to rapidly improve.

I slipped my hands down the front of myself, watching his reaction carefully as my fingers slid through my slick folds.

A low groan fell from Seven's lips, and I smiled. I held my wet fingers up to his lips and spread my cum on them, his tongue immediately slipping out to grab every drop. After he'd gotten a taste, I began to slide my hands down his body, my fingers caressing the scars on his chest, making sure to stay away from the wound that was healing before my eyes. He froze, and there was something unsure in his gaze, something vulnerable as I softly touched his scars. Keeping eye contact with him, I moved forward, softly kissing them. His whole body shook the second my lips grazed his skin, a gasp escaping from his lips. I smiled at the sound and gave his skin one more kiss before shifting back.

Seven moaned loudly as I wrapped my hand around his thick shaft. "I love this," I murmured. My first few strokes were slow and measured. I was transfixed as I stared at his dick, the glistening drop of cum peeking out from his swollen head, the delicious veins standing out in stark relief on his length.

His dick was a work of art.

I began to move my hand faster, up and down, up and down as my gaze shifted to his face, which was flushed with color. Seven's eyes were glued to my hand on his dick, ecstasy all over his features.

"He loves that, sweetheart. You're so good for us," Ash growled softly behind me, and I was so wet I was probably dripping all over Seven's leg.

He didn't seem to mind.

I bent down and licked up the drop of pre-cum, savoring

the taste, and his breath hiccuped as I licked him like he was my favorite candy.

"Fuck," Seven groaned as I began to lap at his slit, desperate to taste more of him.

"Fuck. You smell so good. He's so lucky," Ash purred as my hand continued to move, and as I licked and sucked all over his length.

Seven's head fell back, and his body was rigid as I licked and tongued his slit, savoring every drop. His breathing began to speed up, and I decided that his healing would be much better if I rode him for a bit before he came.

I was generous like that.

The hole in his chest had closed up by now, nothing to show for his near-death experience but a rigid, red scar. Seven didn't seem too worried about his wound at the moment, though. His eyes were desperate twin flames as he watched me scoot forward and line myself up over the top of his length.

I teased him a bit, dragging his tip through my folds, loving how desperate he looked.

"Please," he gasped.

"Please what?" I teased.

"Please fuck me," he begged. It was a heady thing, having this glorious creature literally desperate for me.

Ash chuckled darkly behind me, his breath puffing against my neck. "Don't be mean, sweetheart. He did almost die, after all." His hands went to my hips, gripping and massaging them as Seven stared at me worshipfully.

"Well, I guess when you put it that way." I dropped down on Seven's thick cock slowly, because the stretch was beyond intense. Ash guided my movements.

In my dreams, I'd been with Ash and Seven several times together, but Seven had always been hiding behind me or covering himself up. Having him laid out like this in front of me, with Ash the one behind me...I loved it.

Ash groaned behind me like I'd just hopped on his dick.

"How good does she feel, brother?" Ash purred.

"So good," Seven moaned, his muscles trembling beneath me as he tried to restrain himself from taking over.

I already felt completely stuffed full...when all of a sudden, the pressure inside me multiplied. It felt like he was doubling in size. "What the fuck?" I gasped.

Ash chuckled wickedly behind me. "Oh, perhaps we should have mentioned that. You didn't exactly get the whole dick experience in our dreamland romps. Seven here is a grower."

Grower indeed. I felt so full, it was hard to breathe. He felt like he was pressing up into the entrance of my womb.

"It feels better if you move, sweetheart," Ash murmured as he lifted me up and then slammed me back down on his brother's literal monster dick.

"Yes. Just like that," Seven groaned as Ash began to move me up and down, finding the perfect rhythm and angle to make my eyes roll back and a desperate moan spill from my throat. Ash plastered himself against my back and wrapped one arm all the way around me so he could control my movements, while his other hand moved to my breasts. He began to tug and knead at my breasts, and the pleasure I was feeling was so intense that I honestly didn't recognize the noises coming out of my mouth.

"Use him, sweetheart. Just like he's using you to feed. Choke him with your perfect cunt," Ash continued as Seven writhed underneath me.

Ash pushed me forward so that my clit was rubbing against Seven's cock, and he stopped playing with my breasts, something that Seven excitedly took over. Seven latched onto my left nipple, suckling it into a hard point.

"You're riding him so good, Blake. Sweetest fucking pussy

in all the worlds," Ash growled as his arm continued to move me up and down.

I stared into Seven's violet eyes, watching entranced at the myriad of emotions in their depths. Suddenly...his eyes hardened and his face went blank.

Ash held me still, sniffing the air. "Fuck. The asshole's here. Are you up for taming him?"

I realized that this was one of Seven's other identities. Creed had explained about them the other night. Judging by what I was seeing in his features, this is the one I'd been with in that room.

Seven growled underneath me at Ash's comment and abruptly tore me off his dick and out of Ash's grip, flipping me around so I wasn't facing him anymore before plunging me back down on his dick in a reverse cowgirl style.

And he somehow grew more.

"Can't breathe," I gasped as Seven's sadistic personality began to bounce me ruthlessly up and down his length.

Ash just laughed. "Figures he would try and show off. He's insecure like that," Ash joked.

"Shut the fuck up and fuck her mouth, you fucking pussy," Seven growled from behind me, only making Ash laugh harder.

"My pleasure," Ash grinned before sliding his pants down and revealing his gloriously delicious dick.

I had never thought dicks could be delicious before these beasts had invaded my dreams. I'd been so wrong.

You would never know Ash was blind was all I could think when his dick went right to my mouth without missing or slapping me in the face.

"Open up, sweetheart."

I automatically opened my mouth while Seven continued to rail into me. Ash slid part of his dick in—there was no way that any human girl could fit something that size all the way in, and then began to gently fuck my mouth, praising me continually as I licked and sucked and tried to give him my best work.

Barely a second had passed before my insides began tightening and fluttering, and I came, squeezing Seven's dick even more as the pleasure overwhelmed me.

He gasped and began to rut into me even harder, his rhythm all over the place as he chased his pleasure. Ash's movements also sped up until drool and pre cum were literally dripping down my chin and my eyes were watering from my efforts.

"Such a good girl. Such a fucking good girl," Ash said as Seven roared with his release and flooded my insides with what felt like buckets of cum.

I probably needed to make sure that the birth control shot I'd been given at Bright Meadows worked on monsters. Because if not...I'd table that thought.

The sweet taste of Ash's cum almost choked me as he came without warning, his praising words sending me spiraling into another fantastically amazing orgasm.

Ash slid his length out of my mouth, petting my hair as he told me how incredible I was. My eyes were already drooping as he slid me off his brother and into his arms.

"Don't take her anywhere," Seven's grumpy alter ego barked, and Ash shot me a grin. He slid me into bed next to Seven and then crawled into the bed on my other side.

"Bet you're not feeling like you're going to die anymore," said Ash lightly, even though I could see the relief in his gaze as he stared over me at his brother's chest where the wound had completely disappeared.

Seven grunted, wrapped his arm around my waist, and pulled me closer to him so that his still hard cock was nestled between my cheeks.

"Going to take you right there," he said tiredly as Ash rolled his eyes.

I giggled, but my eyes were already drooping as Ash scooted closer to me.

"Not if I take it first," Ash whispered right before I slipped into dreamland once again.

Chapter 12

Blake

Two days later, I'd fallen into a routine. My monsters had been busy dealing with the kingdom and Gazen troubles apparently—so I'd been waking up and having breakfast with them, and then spending a couple of hours by myself swimming in the lake under the eyes of the watchful guards I'd been assigned. Then I'd have lunch, and I'd end the day either sitting on the balcony staring out at the city or in my room. One night I'd been left alone, and last night, Creed slipped into bed with me to feed...more like give me mind-blowing sex. After which, I slept like a rock.

He mentioned I needed more time to acclimatize to Wyld. But I was desperate to find out more about this city. If I was going to be stuck here, shouldn't I know firsthand what other dangers lurked in the shadows?

My emotions were tangled on exactly how I felt about the whole ordeal, about the monsters, about everything I'd experienced thus far. And could I really live here? I wasn't so sure. But for now, I'd discover as much about Wyld as possible.

With that decision made, I crossed the room and opened

the door quietly. The Minotaur-looking guard set to accompany me anywhere I went was nowhere in sight.

Perfect.

On silent footsteps, I slipped out into the hallway, figuring I'd do some exploring of my own. I'd swiped a fork from lunch as a weapon, just in case, and it was tucked into the pocket of my pants.

The windows revealed a chaotic world outside. A dirty yellow haze spread through the city, choking it, most likely rising from the lava pit beneath us. It still stunned me that Wyld had been constructed over liquid fire. That right there was some crazy shit. And it reminded me to never fall over a balcony. Not that that was a life goal in the first place.

With the circular hallway I followed bringing me back around to my room, I decided to try the elevator.

I stood in the metal box, staring at the panel with no buttons. How many floors did this tower have, anyway? I'd been using it for the balcony, pool, and back, and after wracking my brain, I called out, "Library."

"Lower floor," the raspy elevator voice responded.

Suddenly, the elevator dropped, and my stomach fell right through me because we were going incredibly fast. I might have screamed too as I grabbed onto the walls.

"No, stop," I whined, pinning myself into the corner to avoid falling over. Why in the world did these move so fast? "Library," I tried once more, which did nothing. Okay, there was no such thing in the tower, I guessed.

Panic pressed into me with the notion of flying closer to the lava pit, and I didn't want to discover what monsters kept in their basement.

"Stop," I called out firmly this time.

The elevator came to an abrupt stop, and everything I'd eaten that day churned in my stomach, threatening to come out.

When the doors slid open, I practically threw myself out, gasping for air. That was a damn death trap waiting to happen. What I needed was a manual or schematics of this tower to know what each location was called.

Lifting my gaze, I took in my surroundings.

Skeletal bones were threaded into the mud-like walls. Fiery torches in wall brackets lit up the place that reminded me of some kind of archaeological dig. I made my way to the window to find myself eye to eye with a lower part of the city. Bridges crisscrossed one another, winding around the lofty towers and shorter ones. And all manner of monsters lingered on their balconies. I was talking about beastly things that walked on all fours, eight feet, or more. Most of the creatures that low seemed to resemble insects, including those terrifying spider guards.

Steam rose in waves around them, and I could just imagine how scorching hot it had to be out there.

A wave of heat passed over me as I stared outside, so I made my way down the wide corridor. I studied the monstrous skeletons in the walls that left me shuddering at how creepy they were. One wall panel consisted of just eyes, and I moved quickly onward.

What this place needed was small information labels on what each of these creatures were.

It wasn't long before I found myself standing in front of an arched doorway made of entwined branches. It stood ajar, and I peeked inside.

I gasped aloud instantly and wished I hadn't ended up on this floor.

Severed heads encased in glass hung from the ceiling all around the room like some kind of morbid funhouse.

What the fuck was I looking at?

The door suddenly opened from the inside so abruptly that I lost my footing and stumbled into the room.

Breaths racing, I caught myself before I royally fell right onto my face. Dread laced through my veins as I found the culprit who'd startled me half to death.

A monster who had to be at least nine feet tall, lanky, and dressed in a black pressed suit. His white shirt was buttoned up to his long throat, leading to an elongated head. Skin almost blue, greasy black hair plastered to his head and forehead–the guy reminded me of a zombie.

"Did you have an appointment?" he asked in a gravelly tone, his thin white lips peeling over a row of dagger-like teeth.

"Appointment?"

"I'm certain I didn't have you down in the records." He huffed, the gills along his neck fluttering. He marched right past me in long strides as though he walked on stilts. He moved to the other side of the room and started flickering through a thick, leather book that could easily pass as the Book of the Dead.

My attention was torn between the strange monster and the dangling heads in glass cubes because he was acting so normal in a room where nothing was normal. Definitely not the perfectly preserved heads that had a real-life quality about them. Or the fact that their eyes were open, seeming to stare at me, no matter where I stood.

No surprise, they were all monstrous heads, from one resembling a serpent's head completely with a forked tongue, to a horned beast, another with two mouths, and the list went on with so much weirdness. These weren't the kind of monsters I was attracted to–I seemed to have a type.

The white walls in the long room only added to the creepiness factor.

"No, I don't have you down," the man barked, and I jumped in my shoes. "But perhaps Creed had arranged a tour and forgot to tell me. He sometimes does that." The monster rambled as he treaded back toward me.

"I'm Blake," I stated.

"Of course you are," he replied, smacking his lips. "Everyone knows who you are. We've all drank from your energy." He gave a slight bow of his head. "I'm Boltaroy." Then he smacked a fist to his chest in a war-like manner. "I'm the guardian of all the deceased major political figures who once ruled in the kingdom of Wyld."

He turned toward the heads and started meandering between them. "We respect our leaders, and once they perish, their heads are forever immortalized to be remembered. Take Hake here." He pointed to a creature with a fish head, that had me blinking and attempting not to laugh. "Hake led our first army to war when we established our home."

Boltaroy glanced at me over his shoulder with a furrowed brow. "Keep up. I won't repeat myself on this tour."

"Oh," I gasped. We were on a tour of the freaky head museum apparently. So I hurried behind him, weaving among the heads, learning about generals and commanders who all achieved some kind of greatness through savagery basically.

Then we entered another room, the walls painted with gold. And in the middle was one head encased in glass suspended from the ceiling.

It was a woman with curls framing the most beautiful face. If she was this spectacular dead, I could only imagine how beautiful she'd been in real life. Reddish skin, eyes of the bluest oceans, thorns sticking out of her neck as though it was a necklace. And small silvery horns protruding out of her temples. On top of her head sat a golden crown dripping in a myriad of colored jewels.

"The Red Queen," he announced with pride in his voice. "She reigned over Wyld fiercely, destroying many of our enemies. She fed our nation abundantly."

My mouth dropped open at the thought that this

kingdom once had a queen. Creed called himself King, so did that mean she was his partner?

"She was horribly murdered, and ever since, Creed and his circle have been working tirelessly to feed the people of Wyld."

"Who would kill the queen?"

Boltaroy's face pinched, and he seriously looked traumatized. "We still don't know, but ever since her death, our city has struggled with finding a replacement and ensuring we had enough food."

Thoughts of my past conversations with Creed about feeding his population came to mind, and the more I thought of everything about me feeding everyone and staying here forever... I gasped as reality came to mind.

Was he thinking I could take the queen's place? I blinked at her head in the cube, and I kept seeing myself in there. Most things in Wyld wanted to hurt me. Plus, I was human. I didn't belong in such a place, let alone in any kind of ruling situation.

Nope, that had to be a huge mistake, and maybe I was a stand-in until they found someone of royal blood, right? Then why did something in my chest constrict at the thought of me losing the monsters' attention?

That thought alone startled me, and I nervously tugged at the locks of hair over my shoulder. What was wrong with me? Had I actually allowed my pussy to make decisions based on carnal pleasure?

"And that concludes our tour," Boltaroy suddenly spluttered as he hurried into the other room where I noticed a female equivalent to him entering the room. Someone was trying to score a date.

I was walking around the queen's head when I spotted another entryway. Sure, it had a door, but it *was* slightly open, and I traipsed over into the other room.

Instantly, it felt as though I'd been teleported into a royal chamber, and putting two and two together, told me this had once been the queen's bedroom. Perhaps they changed her room into a museum, or they moved all her furniture down here.

Either way, it was spectacular.

An elaborate bed with bony clawed feet and enormous black bat wings stretching outward from the bedposts against the wall.

More gold walls, along with a matching dresser. All manner of torture contraptions hung off one wall. Someone was into kinky bondage.

Out of curiosity, I made my way to the wardrobe and pulled it open.

Golds, silvers, and blacks stared back at me. They were all elaborate gowns that screamed royalty, and I could just imagine that beautiful queen looking immaculate and looking every part the queen.

I traced my fingers across the glitter sleeve of a coat; the pebbly diamond studs were sharp and they pricked my finger. "Ouch."

Shutting the doors, I made my way to a large study table, layered with an ancient map that had browned at the curling corners. It was a map of the Shadowburn realm.

It was mostly a mass of yellow sand with one circular mass labeled as Wyld in the top left-hand side, while another larger city was on the right side of the map, titled Forsaken.

Well, if that wasn't foreboding, I didn't know what was.

In between the two cities was a smattering of smaller dots without names. So the whole realm only had two major cities, which begged the question... where did they come from originally if the cities had been built by monsters?

Someone cleared their voice behind me, and I startled around, expecting Boltaroy...but it wasn't him.

I froze.

"What are you doing here?" Tempest growled in his

monstrous form, shoulders lifting in an aggressive manner. His broken horn had mostly grown back, so not like he could hold a grudge against me for Creed snapping it. "No one should be in here." His voice climbed.

I trembled because he always put me on edge, especially if he was in a foul mood.

"I-I was on a tour," I answered, then cleared my throat.'

Tempest swallowed the space between us in three long strides. "Each time you disobey our rules, I should punish you. That would only be fitting." That devious smirk split his beautiful lips, but no amount of smiling could hide the fact he was dangerous.

But I also wouldn't let him play me as I'd heard Creed's threat if he hurt me again. That gave me the bravery to respond with, "I suggest saving your lecture for when a rule is broken. As I said, I was on a tour, and that included this room, seeing as the door was open. And not once had I been instructed this room was out of bounds."

The sharp intake of breath followed me, and when I turned around, Tempest was in my face, leaving less than an inch between us.

Ice filled my veins, and I might have ruined any chance of escaping him intact with my big fat mouth, but annoyance had me saying, "Have you heard of personal space?"

"You speak so brazenly to me that I should strip you down, strap you to the walls, and show you real punishment." His voice was cold, and he suddenly seized my arm, long fingers snapping around my wrist.

My leg quivered as his grip tightened. I tugged against him. "Release me."

"You're curious about our queen, I get it, but be careful what lines you're prepared to cross because they will come with consequences," he hissed. A spark of darkness flashed behind his eyes, darkening his green pupils, his form seeming to flicker back and forth between his human and monstrous form.

"What's wrong with finding out about your queen? I wasn't going to disturb anything in her room."

He leaned closer, whispering, "You have your claws out today. Hold onto them; you'll need them because I prefer when you fight back."

I clenched my jaw tight, shaking not only at his threat, but at the lick of arousal slithering across my clit. Tempest had always scared me, but I'd also been having sex with him in my dreams. As such, we'd developed a strange like / hate relationship. And now, even a single touch from him reminded my body of the endless pleasure he'd brought me.

"You can let me go," I stated with conviction behind my words.

He didn't waver, but stared into the depth of my soul, his forked tongue dragging across his bottom lip. "This room is out of bounds," he commanded in my face, trembling with obvious anger. "Don't underestimate me, Blake."

I bit down on my tongue to hold back any kind of reaction. I refused to give him any joy in bringing me agony.

"I know you want me, but it's admirable that you're trying to hold back."

With all my strength, I wrenched my arm out of his grip.

He laughed callously at me. "One warning is all you get," he snarled. "Next time you poke around where you shouldn't, I'll bend you over and fuck you until you pass out, and then I'll keep fucking you so when you wake up, you'll feel sore for a week straight."

A low, breathy gasp expelled past my lips, and I retreated from his side. "I-I should go. Boltaroy will be looking for me to continue our tour."

"She wasn't always the nicest person," Tempest said as I crossed the room, bringing me to a pause.

"Who?" I asked, twisting to look at him now standing next to the bed, staring down at the silky bed sheets in his human form. In that ridiculously handsome guise he wore that was deceiving to anyone who saw it. At first glance, anyone would fall head-over-heels for him, until they discovered there was a devil on the inside.

He glanced up with those piercing emerald eyes, the corners of his mouth tugging awkwardly into a half-grin. It looked wrong on him. "She meant the world to us, you know. She was our world." His gaze fell back to her bed.

How many times had he fallen into bed with the queen? Did I even compare to her? Or was I the poor substitute?

"Her death led to the fall of our kingdom, but it also impacted us all differently. We all still mourn for what we once had. And what had been stolen from us."

I almost believed the heartache in his voice. My breath quickened at the thought that I'd misunderstood Tempest. Did his temper and aggression all boil down to the pain of losing his queen? Did he love her that much?

With his attention returned to the bed, his shoulders curving forward, I retreated from the room hastily, more confused than ever.

Just when I thought I'd understood one of the monsters, they went and messed things up.

Once I left the room, I turned on my heels and ran, not stopping until I reached my room. All the while, I had a feeling that things with Tempest were only going to get worse before they got better.

Chapter 13

Blake

I was bent over a bed, being fucked from behind, Steele's huge cock thrusting in and out of me so fast that the room spun with me.

Gasping for air, I moaned, lifting my ass higher for each plunge. God...the man could fuck hard. And he did so like he owned me. Not in the possessive kind, but like I literally belonged to him.

Wanton, frenzied desire flared through me the harder he slapped into me. "Steele, don't stop, please don't ever stop," I begged with desperation, needing so much more.

My nipples tightened, and I sucked in each ragged breath, my world fading to white as he claimed me, over and over. He'd found a rhythm, an unrelentingly fucking rhythm I drowned in.

I couldn't forget the feelings he awakened in me, or how much I screamed for more.

Hands—or were they claws? —dug sharply into my hips, holding me in place firmly.

"More," I gasped.

164

He paused his assault, and I moaned out of pure sexual frustration. "I was so close," I breathed. "Please. Keep going."

"Give me a moment. I have something else planned to heighten the sensation," he murmured with that sexy voice that drove me wild.

I slowly lifted myself, my drenching pussy leaking down my inner thighs from how incredibly turned on he'd left me. I was a live fuse, and if he lit me up now, I'd go off.

Steele stood in front of me, deliciously naked, his thick, heavy cock glistening from my juices. But my attention fell to the red ribbon dangling from his fingers. In his other hand, he held two, small metallic clamps, connected by a looped chain, and his grin was completely devious.

I swallowed hard, squeezing my thighs at the sight of what he had in store for me. "How does this work?"

"You'll see," he teased, his eyes burning with lust. Something was odd about him, though. He appeared to be twitching, looking like he might vanish before my eyes. Shifting between his spectacular nakedness to something dark and shadowed, I blinked my eyes, unsure if it was just me, or if it was actually happening.

He kept smiling at me as though everything was normal.

"Steele, are you okay?"

"Everything is just as it should be," he instructed me, lifting his hand with the ribbon. "Now be a good girl for me and do what I tell you to do. This is going to feel so good, baby, and it won't be long before I save you."

Confusion flared through my thoughts, unease settling in my muscles.

Nothing seemed to bother Steele, who looked at me like I was his world, and that smile made me forget every worry. Leaning forward, he gently laid the thick ribbon across my eyes and tied it at the back of my head.

He pressed up against me, his fingertips sliding down my

arms. His breath danced on my face, the muscles beneath his skin shifting against me, and a deep growl rolled on his throat.

"Your beauty is unbelievable," he whispered, followed by kisses across my collarbone.

Fingers tipped with what felt like claws gently pressed into my breasts as he cupped them. He took a nipple into his mouth, sucking hard, the sharpness of his canines lightly grazing across the tender flesh.

I flinched at first, not expecting the teeth, then he paid the same attention to my other breast, the pleasure growing on me rather quickly.

"This is going to be a bit cold. Do you trust me?" he asked.

"Of course," my response was instant, with no hesitation. I knew that I trusted Steele instinctively.

"Good. I love seeing you like this, Blake. My cock is so hard, I can barely stand it. I'm going to lose my mind, this image of you forever embedded in my mind."

The cold metal of what I assumed were the steel bars from the clamps were placed over a nipple and slightly tightened.

I moaned at the sensation, from how much a small amount of pressure turned me on. My pussy pulsed, and by the time he secured the second one, I was panting, my thighs pressing together.

"Fucking spectacular. You have no idea how much I love hearing you cry out for more, how much it gets me off knowing I did that to you." His hands fell to my hips. The next thing I knew, I was off my feet and laid on the bed.

The light squeeze of the clamps on my nipples was a tantalizing pain I wasn't exactly used to—blood pounded there, bringing a sensation very different to what his mouth aroused from within me.

His hands slid down my legs to my knees, and every stroke, every flicker of his sharp fingernails, intensified the lustful sensation burning me up. Not being able to see his next move had my pulse leaping into my throat with each touch, my pussy tingling for his next move.

"What now?" I asked, half mischievously.

"I'm going to fuck you like I never have before," he said, leaving me slightly confused. "But first." He drew apart my knees, wider and wider, until I lay on the bed completely splayed out for him, my body tingling all over. "I love seeing you like this, letting me do anything I want to do to you. And look at that pink, delicious pussy, dripping for me."

His words infused me with an exhilarating thrill.

"Please, Steele," I begged, laying on my back, completely in the dark with the ribbon across my eyes. The clamps pinched my nipples just enough to keep me buzzing, and I apparently adored the kinky side of sex. Something the monsters had introduced me to.

There was no fear, only adrenaline-infused desire.

"You're going to wreck me," Steele purred as he pressed his body between my legs. A strange sensation of both warmth and coldness crawled up my legs at his touch. My skin rippled with goosebumps, yet I pushed my hips up to meet him, eager to have him back inside me.

Blood pounded in my ears, thumping in my veins, his teasing leaving me burning up and restless.

His hands traveled to my waist, and he hoisted me closer to him; instantly, the bulge of his cock rubbed against my entrance.

"I'm going to fuck you on the bed first, and then I'll take you against the wall, sticking out the window...every fucking place so there isn't a spot left here where I haven't rutted you."

"Then do it already," I challenged. "Because right now, it's not fair that I don't get to see you."

He laughed, and I worshiped the sound he made. "Nothing's fair, sweetheart. All that matters is how much I love you. You are my everything," he whispered with a possessive growl, then he plunged into me.

It came without a warning, and I screamed, my back arching from how hard he'd buried himself into me. He somehow stretched me wider than the last time we'd fucked, impossibly so where he filled every inch of me, stretching me to that blissful point where pain and pleasure tangled into an unbelievable sensation.

I gasped for air at how much he pulled me apart, but there was no stopping him either. This gorgeous, muscular man took me harder, every touch, every friction caused by our bodies bursting like sparks across my skin. The roughness of his body kept me locked to him, taking what he wanted without pause.

I lost track of how long he fucked me, but I'd given myself to him completely.

"I'm all yours, Steele," I cried out while he assaulted me with his savagery. I ached to pull the blindfold off to stare into his face while I throbbed with desire.

Then I felt something strange deep within me, as though his huge cock vibrated. But that couldn't be right. A thousand questions spun around in my head, stolen as quickly as they came by how fast he fucked me—if that was even possible. The whole bed rocked back and forth, my breaths racing.

I cried out with an insane amount of pleasure as he took every inch of me, bringing me so close to the edge, and I knew the climax would blow my mind.

My nipples hurt in the clamps with how hard they pebbled, and the sensation of not seeing him played on my mind.

"Blake, I'm never going to stop this. I can't. All I think about, day and night, is rutting you, filling your cunt with so much cum that you'll breed for me. I need this, fuck," he growled, and I felt an added pressure as his cock somehow grew and wildly vibrated inside me.

My teeth were chattering. And just when I thought I couldn't take anymore, a jolt of pleasure tore through me so violently, I screamed.

"That's it," Steele moaned, thrusting deep before pausing as he came, pulsing. The heat of his cum flooded me.

The whole time I screamed, my body shuddered, falling apart, and I couldn't stand it any longer. I ripped off the ribbon from my eyes, needing to see him.

And my screams of pleasure morphed into ones of terror.

Because instead of Steele, I was being claimed by a huge monster, black mist dancing around him, glowing eyes and a mouth filled with knife-like teeth.

And he looked at me—like he was ready to eat me.

I jolted out of sleep with a scream, finding myself in my bed completely alone. Sweat trickled down my neck, hair stuck to the sides of my face. I was getting extremely tired of constantly waking up in this crazed state.

Back on Earth, I'd dreamed of monsters fucking me. Now in their realm, I'd started imagining humans were monsters.

I'd clearly been having too much sex because it had infused into every inch of my life.

MOST OF THE day passed in a blur. I was completing my last lap of the lake, since I'd been challenging myself to swim more each day...only to realize I wasn't alone.

Pausing in the cool waters, I turned around to find Ash and Seven standing by the bank, twins who looked nothing alike in their monster or human forms. Right now, they were in their monster forms. Behind them, Freddy was standing next to a long table that reminded me of the ones at the massage parlors.

"What's going on?" I asked.

"We have a surprise for you," Seven said, a softer expression capturing his eyes, and I figured he was in a better mood today.

"What he's trying to say," Ash butted in, "Is that he's trying to make it up to you for being a fucktard to you the other day."

"Oh," I said, treading water.

Seven might have been blushing, but it was impossible to see with the mask he wore over the bottom half of his face and his hood. One day, I'd have to ask him why he covered himself up. "It was Ash's suggestion. I just organized it," he finally said.

"And what is it?" I kept eying Freddy suspiciously.

"Come out," Ash said. "And find out."

Swimming over to the edge, I climbed out in my substitute swimsuit–black underwear and tank top.

They both walked over to Freddy who looked especially awkward with all his globbiness.

"Freddy is going to give you a back massage," Ash announced, sounding rather pleased with himself. "Humans love those."

A strange sound must have fallen past my lips as they all stared at me strangely.

"She doesn't like it," Seven blurted.

"No, it's not that; I love massages," I said a bit too quickly. That was going to be my excuse, hating massages, but I'd panicked when I saw their depressed faces. "I'm just a bit surprised."

"She doesn't sound convincing," Freddy stated.

"Oh, she wants it," Ash said, grabbing my arm and gently lifting me up and laying me on my stomach on the long table.

"This is the perfect location," Seven added. "Cool breeze, the shade of the trees, and no one to stare at you."

My heart was beating ridiculously because I wasn't sure how I felt about this at all. But before I could even protest, Ash used one of his claws to rip my tank off me.

I squeaked with shock and grasped onto the wooden table.

The next thing I knew, something icy cold and gelatinous landed on my back. I screamed a bit that time, my body flinching at the cold.

"Fuck, Freddy," Seven growled. "I told you to be tender."

"Of course, master. I've never massaged a human before."

"Maybe one of you should, ahhh," I moaned at the sudden application of suction cups to my back from Freddy who clearly has octopus-like arms beneath his gloppy form.

I gripped the table still, unsure how to feel about the jelly sensation running across my back, though after a while, there was something slightly enjoyable about the pressure of the suction cups across my shoulder blades. I held my stress there.

Ash and Seven stood on the side, facing me as I rested my cheek on the table, my body bouncing about from the strange-ass massage.

"Thank you," I said. "It was thoughtful of you."

"We used to receive regular messages. I preferred to be walked on and have my back cracked," Ash explained. "Ahh, those were the days before everything went to shit."

Seven never spoke, but stared at me intensely, and it was always hard to tell what he was thinking or how he'd react. At least with Tempest, it was clear he would always be an ass, so I could deal with that. But Seven was unpredictable.

In that same moment, my thoughts circled on what Ash had said, and with it, I remembered what I'd learned about the queen on my recent tour of the room with heads.

"I hope it's not rude of me to ask, but did they even find out who killed her?"

Freddy's movement paused across my back before starting up again, kneading me a lot harder. I shifted around on the table, hoping he'd get the message to back down.

Ash shrugged as though the news was old, except I caught the quickening of his breath. Seven remained the epitome of a statue, so it surprised me when he replied, "The traitor was in our ranks, one of our own. A fifth monster who'd been in Creed's circle. He was actually the closest to Creed, so it was especially devastating. He was the last one with the queen the night she was butchered. And conveniently, he ran away afterward and hasn't been seen since."

"He's guilty," Ash added. "Why the fuck would he run if he had nothing to hide?"

"And you haven't searched for him?"

"Steele had always been a slippery prick, and he'd hidden—"

My head grew dizzy instantly, my pulsing heartbeat in my ears blocking out the rest of his words. Had I heard right? Could it be the same person?

Unease rattled me, leaving me in a state of shock.

"Wait, come again." I pushed myself up, brushing Freddy aside, and sat on the edge of the table. "What did you say his name was?"

"Steele," Ash repeated. "A fucking traitor, and when we catch him, he's going to wish he'd died instead of the queen." He cocked his head, realizing I was acting strange. "Have you heard the name before?"

The world seemed to rush around me, and I stopped breathing for a moment. With it came the dream from this morning and Steele morphing into a monster. I didn't want to believe it because other people were named Steele too, right?

My memories flashed through my head, my heart stuttering that they could possibly be talking about the same man I'd fallen for back at the asylum. The man who'd paid me visits in my dreams... just as the monsters had done back on Earth.

His words kept humming over my mind.

I'm coming to find you, sweetheart.

Suddenly, everything felt too much... way too much.

I was going to throw up, so I hopped down from the table and grabbed a towel from the ground to cover myself. My words came out barely a whisper, "I want to go back to my room, please. I'm not feeling well."

How I got back to my room was a blur. My insides were ice...I didn't want to believe it was my Steele. It had to be a terrible mistake.

I attempted to feel my own emotions while my heart constricted the longer I thought about it. I had feelings for Steele, but was he a killer, hiding on Earth?

Sliding onto my bed and pulling my knees up to my chest, I kept telling myself it had to be a terrible coincidence. A mistake.

Because I knew the real Steele.

Didn't I?

Chapter 14

Blake

The mood was somber when I arrived at breakfast the next morning, and I looked at everyone worriedly. What had happened?

I slid into my chair, thanking Freddy when he set down something that resembled oatmeal, a pile of those chocolate leaves on a small plate next to the bowl. My mouth watered just looking at them. They could make anything taste good. I went to take a bite, but then set my spoon down when I saw that even Ash looked upset. And Ash almost never looked upset.

"What's going on?" I asked warily.

Creed's lips pursed like he was debating whether to tell me, but I could always count on Tempest for some bad news.

"We're not producing enough for Wyld," he snapped.

"Producing enough of what?"

"Food...energy...sex," Creed interjected, shooting Tempest a glare.

Well, that was alarming. I was throbbing between my legs right now from how hard Ash had taken me that morning.

"Um, exactly how much sex are you thinking it takes?"

It was hard to keep myself from asking how often they'd fucked their queen for her to keep the whole city fed. I definitely didn't want to know the answer to that, but it was tempting.

"It's not the strength of the lust you're producing, it's just how far it's traveling. It's like there's an invisible wall in parts of the city that is preventing all of Wyld from being fed," explained Ash, obviously trying to make me feel better.

Although, I didn't know why I was feeling bad in the first place. It was almost like I was starting to care about the monsters of Wyld.

"I have an idea," announced Tempest, drawing our attention to where he'd stood up suddenly from the chair. Everyone looked at him expectantly.

"Pariah."

"No. Absolutely not," snarled Seven and Ash almost simultaneously. Their gazes locked on Creed.

"Creed. You can't be serious," said Ash.

Dread flickered in my gut as I turned to look at Creed. He was sitting in his chair, one of his long pointed claws tapping on his chin thoughtfully.

"Explain," he ordered Tempest.

"Pariah sits in the very epicenter of Wyld. Energy has always been collected there, even when the Red Queen was alive. We all know there's something different about those coordinates. We fuck her there...it could be amplified."

"What's Pariah?" I asked, fiddling with the napkin in my lap.

"It's closest to what humans call..." Creed began.

"A sex club," finished Ash, looking enraged.

"You want to take me to a sex club?"

Tempest looked smug when he answered me. "It would hardly be the craziest thing we've done to your body, Blake."

I opened my mouth to argue with him, but he was probably right.

Except there was definitely a difference between crazy group sex...and crazy public sex.

"Rachidra is pregnant," said Creed abruptly.

All the men gasped.

"Drakon sent me a message this morning."

"When is she due?" asked Ash, looking...terrified.

"In a month's time. Drakon didn't want to tell anyone. He's been beside himself."

"Why do you all look so horrified about that?" I asked.

"Not a single female in Wyld has been able to have a child since..." answered Creed, an edge of melancholy in his voice.

"Since she died," finished Tempest, his gaze burning as he looked at me.

"But I thought you were feeding off of fear and then...my dreams," I asked.

"It wasn't strong enough for some reason. We were able to feed everyone by fucking you for those years, but the Wyld females were still unable to carry a baby to full term," explained Seven.

"Oh," I murmured, a tendril of sadness threading through my insides thinking of all those poor females. "I'm so sorry."

"We have to try Pariah," urged Tempest.

I bit my lip, thinking it over. It's not like Wyld didn't know I was here, getting thoroughly fucked by their leaders. Would it be that different for them to actually see the fucking?

Yes. Yes, it would.

An image flickered in my head just then of myself...round with child. I pushed it away, but the damage had been done.

"I'll do it," I announced softly. Ash looked like he wanted to grab me and run away, and Seven was staring at me inscrutably.

But Creed's face looked perfectly blank. He abruptly got

up from his chair and began to stride out of the room with heavy footsteps. "Be ready in one hour," he growled before he disappeared.

I looked at the three remaining monsters at the table. "How exactly does someone get ready for a monster sex club?"

By WEARING LEATHER, evidently.

Monster sex clubs must be similar to fetish clubs in the human world, because I wasn't sure that the scraps of leather I was wearing right then constituted clothing. My nipples were covered, barely. And my vagina had a leather covering on it, but the rest of my outfit basically consisted of leather straps.

I honestly might as well have been naked.

The guys were wearing some sort of leather loincloth getups that barely covered their dangly bits and their ass cheeks, in their full monster forms. I had to admit they looked perversely sexy. Why I was beyond attracted to them when the rest of the monsters made my stomach hurt didn't make very much sense, but it was the truth.

We had wound our way across what felt like a million bridges by that point, and I was really thinking that they should invest in some kind of transportation besides walking. Just as I opened my mouth to ask how much further we had to go, we rounded a corner, and there in front of us was what must have been Pariah.

The building was made of a similar black ashy stone as the rest of the city, but this building's architecture resembled a gothic Greek cathedral, with columns and a domed top. You couldn't see between the columns into the interior of the building, however. There was a red cloudy glow that hung eerily in the spaces between, blocking any view inside. The ground was pulsing slightly as we walked across the powdery gray dirt-covered road, a haunting beat sounding from the building in front of us.

I felt like I was going to throw up.

Ash was holding onto my hand in a death grip, sending me concerned looks every couple of moments. Seven hadn't looked at me at all. Creed looked like he wanted to kill someone. And Tempest...well, he looked excited.

Bastard.

As we got closer to the building, a dark opening appeared in the walls and one of the creepy spider guards came scuttling out, bending its legs down low so it could bow to Creed.

"This is a surprise, sir. We weren't expecting you," he said in a hissy, scratchy voice that slid down my spine like nails on a chalkboard.

"How's the crowd tonight?" snapped Creed in response. The spider creature took a few steps back, staying bowed low, obviously taken off guard by the venom in Creed's voice. The monster king was not a happy camper at the moment.

"Packed, as usual, sir. The latest attack has made everyone want to let off some steam."

Creed huffed in response and then strode towards the black opening without another word to the...spider bouncer? That was kind of what he was, wasn't it?

Tempest followed Creed, and Ash led me after them, Seven flanking our backs.

You couldn't see anything past the black nothingness that had appeared in the wall, and cold tendrils caressed my skin as we walked through it. I was about to start panicking, even with Ash holding onto me tight, and then the darkness abruptly disappeared...and we popped out into a swirling, sexual nightmare.

We were in an enormous room that seemed far larger than the building had looked capable of having from the outside. Everything was shrouded in a dark red light, and there was red smoke being pumped into the room from the walls.

And there were monsters...everywhere.

Dragon-looking monsters, gooey-looking monsters, a monster that had the head of a boar except with violet tusks protruding out of its face. There were clear tubes pulsing with red light hanging from the ceiling that went to the floor in a winding pattern. Male and female monsters were swinging... naked from the tubes, somehow traveling in circles up and down the thirty-foot ceilings with ease. I was seeing a lot of dicks...and boobs.

I had the weird desire to put my hands over the guys' faces so they couldn't see. Because a lot of these monster girls were beautiful.

I'd been distracted by the pole dancing monsters so I'd somehow missed all the other stuff happening on the outer edges of the room.

All the sex stuff.

My mouth dropped as I saw a female monster with a strap on fucking the living hell out of another female, beating her on the sides of her body with her giant purple bat-looking wings. There were at least five male monsters fucking in sync in a caterpillar formation. There were two monsters with three heads sharing a pretty pink monster with translucent skin.

It was a lot to take in, and I could feel the flush of embarrassment in my cheeks from seeing so much...sex.

I was also feeling very aroused at the moment. All I could hope was that the leather in front of my va-jay was waterproof and not displaying how soaking wet I was to the whole room. It was bad enough that I knew they could probably all smell me.

Ash growled very uncharacteristically at a monster that resembled a praying mantis a few feet away, and the monster scurried away. "What was that for?" I murmured.

"He was looking at you," he said through sharp gritted teeth.

A chuckle slipped out of Seven from behind us. "How did you even know?" I asked...since he was blind.

"I could feel it," Ash said simply, like that was a good enough explanation.

"Okay, so where are we doing this?" I asked nervously, trying to avert my eyes from, well...everything. And really just wanting to get it over with.

"Up there," Tempest said, an excited gleam in his gaze, as he pointed up to a large platform I hadn't noticed yet that was hanging above the dancers...right in the middle of the room.

Before anyone could respond to his idea, three scantily clad monster girls came rushing up to us.

"Your majesty," one of them breathed, her skin a pretty light blue color, small gills on the sides of her neck. Other than that, she looked almost human.

Creed looked at the bar as if she hadn't addressed him. "I think Blake could benefit from a drink," he said as he began to stride towards it. "Don't let her out of your sight," he barked to the others.

Seven growled like he was personally affronted by Creed's reminder, but Ash just laughed exasperatedly.

The girls crowded closer after Creed left, although the blue girl was staring after him hungrily.

Something that felt an awful lot like jealousy unfurled in my chest. I turned away from them, examining the room closer to try and distract myself...

I mean, they wouldn't be interested in those girls, right? The insecurity I was suddenly feeling was maddening.

A pair of arms curled around me, and I sank back against the hard chest, immediately recognizing Ash's touch. One of the girls laughed behind us, and I stiffened.

"What's wrong, sweetheart?" Ash purred in my ear, the

soft touch of his breath reminding me of the other night, sending shivers down my spine.

"Nothing," I said, much too quickly.

"Get the fuck away from me," snapped Seven from behind us, and I found myself relaxing when Seven appeared in my side vision.

Ash chuckled knowingly behind me. "Someone's jealous, brother."

"Jealous?" asked Seven, sounding completely confused.

"I don't know what you're talking about," I replied haughtily.

Ash pulled me in even closer. "Don't be jealous, little one. You're all we see," he whispered.

The spark of jealousy morphed into butterflies softly beating against my insides, because fuck...why had that sounded so amazing?

Tempest sighed loudly behind us, and I pulled away from Ash's comforting embrace to look at him. The girls were gone, and Tempest was staring exasperatedly at the bar where Creed was talking to the bartender...and a small crowd of monsters who'd gathered around him. There was a tray loaded down with drinks right in front of him, presumably for us. "Why on earth did Creed think it would be fast for him to grab the drinks?"

Ash snorted, clapping Tempest on the shoulder. "Let me go grab the drinks at least. You know Creed can't go anywhere without everyone wanting to tell him all their problems for him to solve."

Ash ambled over to the bar, and I might have stared at his ass for a little bit too long because when I did finally manage to tear my gaze away, Tempest and Seven were both staring at me in amusement. Ash was back just a few minutes later with our tray of drinks, Creed still surrounded at the bar, looking like he was about to start punching people if it lasted too much longer.

The drinks on the tray were glowing in a myriad of neon colors. One of the drinks in a tall thin glass was actually changing colors as I watched--first purple, then yellow, then blue. "For my lady," said Ash, handing me a brilliant pink one before passing a glowing green one to Tempest, a blue and orange one to Seven, and keeping the color-changing drink for himself.

"Bottoms up," said Tempest, watching me as he threw back his drink, sparks flaming in his gaze.

"Are you sure this isn't radioactive?" I asked, staring at my glass dubiously.

All three of them looked at me confused. "Okay, that must not be a word you've come across while scaring humans and watching them have sex," I teased as I took a deep breath and took a sip of my drink.

A flavor that was a mix between strawberries and bananas hit my tongue, and I moaned delightedly as I swallowed, jumping when a shock slid down my spine. My body immediately began to feel light and happy, and the garish red light didn't seem nearly as intimidating.

"Um, Ash, what drink did you give her?" Seven asked, cocking his head as he stared at me in alarm. I smiled at him goofily. I just loved him so much.

"You love him, huh?" asked Ash huskily, his eyes beginning to glow. "What about me?"

Sigh. I loved him too.

"Creed, what the fuck did you order?" snapped Tempest as Creed appeared, finally back from the bar. Why did he seem so distressed?

"Creed, you're back, honey," I purred, lurching forward and trying to throw my arms around Creed's neck. Except...he was so fucking tall. Maybe if I climbed him?

"I thought the pink one was just ethernium. She shouldn't have felt it at all," commented Ash, but I wasn't following what they were talking about anymore—I just wanted Creed to hold me.

"Honey. I like that," murmured Creed as he finally gave me what I wanted and picked me up. I nuzzled against his cheek. He was so handsome. My handsome monster. Mine. Mine. Mine.

I heard the rest of them chuckling, and I frowned as I tried to think of a way I could hold all of them at once.

Seven yanked my drink out of my hand just as I was about to take another sip, and I frowned at him, wondering why lilac sparks were dancing around his head. He sniffed at the drink. "Smells like ethernium," he muttered, before taking a sip. "Fuck," he said as he swallowed, his gaze turning dreamy as he stared at all of us and took another long drink.

"I love you guys," he said after a moment in the cutest, softest voice I could imagine.

"You've got to be shitting me," snapped Tempest, ripping the drink out of Seven's hand and throwing it to the ground. He stalked towards the bar.

"Where's he going?" I sighed as I began to smother Creed's face with kisses, loving the way his chest was rumbling with laughter against me.

I felt a warm body behind me and sighed when Seven began to nuzzle my neck. I loved getting this type of attention from him. I moaned and Creed stiffened against me. He gently extricated my arms from around his neck and pushed me into Seven's arms. "What's wrong?" I asked Creed even as Seven and I began to cuddle and exchange kisses.

"I have a lot of self-discipline, pet. But you making those noises and rubbing up against me is one way to break that discipline fast," he explained. I huffed and heard Ash snort.

Seven licked the side of my cheek, and I giggled. "I wish

you could always be like this," I said with a sigh as I ran my hands through his hair. "I love you...like this."

"Crazy about you, sweetheart," Seven purred.

"The ethernium bottle was spiked," Tempest said with a huff as he stomped up to me, tipping up my chin and looking into my eyes.

"Spiked?" asked Creed with a frown.

"Someone put fenderroot in it. There was residue on the inside of the bottle that hadn't dissolved."

"Well, that explains this," Ash said, amused. "We might as well leave. Fenderroot takes hours to wear off. We're just lucky that Seven's not trying to fuck her on the floor right now."

"That sounds wonderful," I sighed as Seven nibbled on my neck.

Creed's laugh floated around me, cocooning me in its warmth.

"We don't need to leave. It will just make her more comfortable," I heard Tempest insist as Seven slipped a finger underneath the small covering over my nipple, softly rubbing it.

"More," I insisted, rubbing up against his hard dick that I could feel underneath his covering.

"Alright, you two," said Ash, grabbing me out of Seven's arms. Seven growled and tried to pull me back. "This isn't happening tonight, Tempest. Get your head out of your ass."

Ash began to stalk towards the entrance as I began to play with his hair, staring over his shoulder at the others. Seven followed us, his gaze locked on me as if I was the center of his universe. It was a heady feeling. I held out my hand to him, wanting him to be closer. I wanted them all to be closer.

Tempest was arguing with Creed about something, but I was starting to get hot...and achy.

I began to rub against Ash more, trying to get pressure on my clit. "I'm hurting," I whimpered into Ash's ear.

"Fuck," he cursed as he turned back to the others. "Hurry the fuck up. It's getting worse."

Tempest snarled while Creed and Seven came after us.

I began to cry when Ash held me still against him. "Why are you doing this to me? Why don't you want me?" I sobbed. Something in the back of my mind was telling me how ridiculous I was acting, but I couldn't help it.

"She's crying. Fuck me," Ash moaned to the others. "Sweetheart, of course I want you. I always want you," he said soothingly, rubbing my ass in a way that only made me hornier.

"I'm going to die if I don't fuck her right now," growled Seven, lunging towards me. Creed caught him around the waist, stopping him an inch away from me.

"Alright, lover boy....let's get you both home. No one is fucking anyone," said Creed exasperatedly. Tempest scoffed next to him, and I realized he was sporting a black eye. When had that happened?

We made it outside, but getting away from the sexual, haunting beat of the club didn't do anything to soften the overwhelming madness I was feeling. I needed to be fucked. Hard. Everywhere.

"Please help me," I moaned, my hands digging into Ash's shoulders in distress.

Seven was struggling against Creed, trying to get to me, and I watched in a daze as Creed pressed something on Seven's neck, causing him to slump over and almost fall to the ground.

"Now we have to carry the bastard home," griped Tempest, shaking his head.

"I can't take it anymore. I have to help her," said Ash helplessly as I continued to sob.

"We are never leaving the castle again," growled Creed, as he looked around at the buildings surrounding us. "Over there," he motioned to an alleyway.

185

"Why don't we just take her back to the club?" said Tempest. "What's the difference?"

"Because others would see her," snapped Ash vehemently, his voice filled with fire. Tempest and Creed looked taken aback at the harsh tone in his voice, and I was even able to stop crying for a minute as I stared in awe at his beautiful, beautiful face.

"No one is seeing her like that but us," Ash snarled, daring any of the others to argue with him. Seven was slung over Creed's shoulder, so he obviously didn't have anything to say... but neither did the others.

"Any monster that sees her getting fucked outside of our circle is going to get their eyes torn out. Am I making myself clear?"

I moaned at that, and a snort slipped from Ash, his face softening from the fierce mask he'd been wearing. "You like my crazy side, sweetheart?" he asked, brushing my hair softly out of my face.

Another rush of lust chose that moment to appear. I was so wet that I could feel drops of my desire on his naked chest since I was wrapped around him like a koala, my pussy flush against his skin.

Ash took off almost at a run down the alleyway, pressing me against the wall as soon as we were hidden from view and devouring my lips. "You smell so fucking good. I bet you taste as good too. So I'm going to give myself a little treat, and take the edge off until we can get you home...sound good?"

"Please!" I begged.

Without making me wait a second more, Ash dropped to his knees, ripped the stupid piece of leather from my aching cunt, and began to devour me. Sucking and licking, his tongue delved into my folds as he slid a thick finger inside me.

"Yes, yes, yes," I chanted, faintly aware of Creed and Tempest watching me with hungry eyes.

Ash slid another finger in, and at that point I was gone, riding his face, desperate for more of his tongue and his touch. Ash's free hand squeezed my ass cheeks, urging me forward.

I loved how Ash gave head. Like it was his favorite thing. Like he could do it all day, every day.

Yes, please.

"You taste so fucking good," Ash said against my skin as he gave my folds another long lick at the same time that he inserted a third finger. I gasped and closed my eyes at how full I felt, even though I knew it wasn't nearly as big as any of them.

"Ride his face, pet. Take what you need," growled Creed, and evidently, his gravely, rough voice was all that I needed, because a second later, I was cumming so hard that I saw stars.

Ash removed his fingers from inside me, but still continued to lick and suck my pussy feverishly, obviously trying to get every drop. His efforts paid off as another orgasm quickly followed the first, less intense but still so fucking good.

He gave me one more long lick before standing up and pulling me back into his arms.

I closed my eyes and snuggled against his shoulder, the raging heat replaced with a pleasant ache that told me I could definitely go for another round—preferably with his cock— but I wasn't going to burst into flames if I didn't get it right away.

"Her smell is everywhere. We need to get the fuck home before all the monsters of Wyld come out and try to play," rumbled Creed as we began to move again.

"Thank you, everyone, for the erection I get to enjoy on our walk back," growled Tempest.

Creed scoffed. "Like you're the only one." I opened my eyes tiredly to see him shifting a still limp Seven on his shoulder. "At least you don't have to carry this one."

"Thank you, Ash," I said softly, snuggling into his neck and taking large inhales of his delicious smell.

"Always, sweetheart. Always," he said.

I relaxed and enjoyed the ride in his arms, all the way home.

Fuck. I really was starting to think of it as home.

"Baby," Steele's *voice murmured as he gently stroked my cheek. I moaned and opened my eyes, only to see him leaning over me. His ice-blue gaze filled with love.*

"You're here," I said softly, feeling achy and feverish.

"What happened to you?" he asked, his voice concerned.

I shifted in my bed, biting down on my lip to try and control the urge to start humping him. "We were at a club, and there was a drink, I think." My voice was gravelly and lust-filled, almost unrecognizable. "I'm really not sure."

"Fuck. They aren't taking care of you at all," he growled, his gaze tracking my hands as they drifted down my body to my aching core.

"Have they given you anything to help, baby?"

I whimpered. "Nothing. I need more, Steele," I begged.

He sighed and squeezed his eyes closed briefly before opening them back up. His hand combed through my hair and I purred at the sensation.

"You need me. They're too distracted right now. You need someone who only cares about you."

"Mmmh. That sounds good," I said dreamily before another pang of lust hit me hard. I cried out and looked up at him beseechingly.

"It's okay sweetheart, I'll take care of you," he murmured as his hands drifted down from my hair, stroking my skin as he made his way to my...

THE NEXT MORNING, it felt like I'd been hit by a wooden beam. Last night was a shit show. Although I'd lasted the rest of the way home without any *services* from the others, I'd needed to be thoroughly fucked by Ash, Creed, and Tempest before I could fall asleep again. I distinctly remembered dreaming about Steele and getting *help* from him. And then I'd finally been given some sort of concoction by Freddy after I'd woken up in the early morning hours and been found trying to mount the "artwork" on the wall–I wasn't going to live that down any time soon.

It felt like I had a hangover—or at least how I imagined it would feel to have a hangover. I'd been trapped in an asylum for my formative years, and been closely watched by my parents before then. So I'd never had a chance to get drunk the way my counterparts had.

My head was pounding, and I felt like puking as I walked down the hall to the dining room. I'd realized pretty quickly that breakfast was some kind of morning ritual for Creed. His kind ate while socializing, but it obviously didn't do much since they needed other types of energy to actually feed. But Creed obviously liked having everyone together in the morning before the day started.

It was kind of cute.

Or—it was usually cute when my head didn't feel like it was going to explode.

Creed, Tempest, and Ash were already seated at the giant black table, eating something that looked like a hunk of raw meat...I was definitely not going to examine it closer.

"Hey there, party girl," Ash called out as soon as he saw me. I flinched at how loud his voice sounded right now. Just seeing his smug, beautiful face had my cheeks flushing a thousand shades of red. As out of my head as I'd been last night, I could clearly remember every single thing I'd done. It felt like watching a stranger when I thought about it, like I was seeing some other girl beg and plead for an orgasm...but it had definitely been me.

I waved shyly and scampered over to my chair. Before I got there though, Creed reached out and pulled me into his lap, rubbing his cheek against mine.

"Good morning, pet," he said huskily, and wouldn't you know, lust evidently fed me just like it did the monsters because I all of a sudden wasn't feeling nearly as sick.

"Hi," I murmured, still blushing but gladly soaking up all the affection the monster king was giving me. I could feel Tempest and Ash's rapt attention on us even as Freddie slid around setting dishes on the table around us.

"I'm sorry about last night. Evidently, there was a shipment of that drink that all came spiked. It's being dealt with."

I shifted in Creed's lap, and he groaned softly, hardening underneath me. I chose to ignore it...because I was classy.

Or at least that's what I was telling myself after last night's debacle.

"What exactly was in that drink?" I asked.

"Ethernium. It's kind of like...that pill that humans in your dance clubs are so fond of. But monster strength."

"Ecstasy? I was drugged with monster Ecstasy last night? Is it alright that I took that?" I rushed out.

Monster Ecstasy made a lot of sense since I'd felt ready to fuck for hours after just a little bit of that drink.

Seven appeared in the doorway, his hair a mess, dark circles under his violet eyes.

"Hey sunshine," Ash chirped.

"Fuck off," Seven growled, staggering to his seat like he was about to pass out at any moment...or throw up. It was hard to tell.

"Here, sir," Freddie mumbled, offering him a dark brown

drink that looked a bit like chocolate milk.

Seven threw it back without question, his color immediately beginning to look better.

"Um, can I have some of that?" I asked, watching what was obviously a crazy good hangover cure.

"I would rather you not," answered Creed, an apology in his eyes at my obvious disappointment. "I have no idea what that would do to a human, and I don't want to make what you're feeling even worse."

Unfortunately, that made a lot of sense. Look what Monster Viagra had done to me last night. Holding off on experimentation sounded pretty good.

"Give her your fucking surprise," growled Seven, a faint flush to his cheeks as he watched me carefully. I wondered what memory he was thinking about from last night. He'd been so fucking sweet. So very un-Seven like.

Ash perked up. "Oh, that should help you feel a bit better!" He jumped up from his seat and practically ran out of the room. It was still amazing how well he sensed everything. I ran into walls all the time, and I was able to see.

"What have you done to my monsters, pet?" asked Creed, his chest rumbling deliciously as he laughed at Ash's eagerness.

I shrugged my shoulders.

"What are you doing to me?" he murmured softly, and my whole insides felt melty and squishy.

Ash appeared a moment later holding a jug of familiar-looking orange liquid. I immediately perked up in Creed's lap. Was that—

"We got you orange juice," Ash announced proudly. "Well, technically, Seven helped, but since he's being such a little asshole this morning, I'm going to take all the credit."

Seven scoffed and rolled his eyes, but there was an amused glint to his gaze as he fondly watched his brother walk over to me.

Creed picked up a fancy-looking glass that I definitely hadn't seen them use before, and Ash went to pour the orange juice.

Just as he began to pour, the city alarms went off, so loud and sudden that Ash missed the cup when he jumped, spilling the juice all over the floor.

"Fuck," he cursed.

Freddy slid in then, looking panicked, or as panicked as a gelatinous glob could look.

"He's been seen, sires," he screeched. "Steele has been seen inside the gates!"

Everyone was up on their feet in an instant, urgency and hatred thick in the air.

My stomach churned with the news. Steele was here? Was it my Steele, or a monster with the same name?

"At last," purred Tempest. Seven and Ash looked furious, while Creed...he just looked shaken at the news.

"Freddy, take Blake to her room and lock the door. No one goes in or out. Do you understand?" Creed barked.

"Yes. I will make sure she is safe," he responded quickly. "I'll alert some of the guards to come up as well."

Creed nodded, but he was obviously already lost in his head, planning what he was going to do.

"Freddy, now!" Seven snapped, and then I found myself set on the floor, Freddy hustling me out of the room, the gleam of his teeth enough to keep me moving. No one said anything to me as I left; they were already striding out of the other exit in the room.

I was pushed down the hall and into my room, Freddy locking the door behind me without a word.

I ran to the window and looked out at the city, my insides trembling, wondering if my Steele was out there right then.

And dreading what would happen if he was.

Chapter 15

Blake

I'd been pacing, utterly beside myself, when someone cleared their voice from within my room.

I froze, because I was of the impression I'd been alone once Freddy had ushered me into my room, locking me in there.

Apparently I was mistaken.

My skin crawled, and I twisted in the direction of the sound just as someone stepped out of the shadows of my walk-in closet.

His ice-blue eyes were the first thing I saw, followed by the piece of his hair that always fell into his beautiful face.

"Steele," I mouthed, shaking down to my core. I felt like I might pass out at seeing him in my room. My doctor from the asylum, the man I'd let myself fall head over heels for, stood in front of me in the monsters' realm.

My stomach clenched, and my heart shuddered.

"My beautiful angel," he said with a smile, his voice gruff and delicious just as I remembered. My heart fluttered in my chest at the sight of him, at the memories of how easily I'd given myself to him. How desperately I'd craved him back on Earth, and in my dreams.

"I missed you," he said, then winked, and my knees weakened. I still couldn't believe how handsome Steele was, from his messy hair that made me want to run my fingers through it, to the way he studied me like a predator stalking his prey. "I told you I'd come for you."

Before I could make sense of anything, my body had already betrayed me. I was running into his arms, and he lifted me off my feet, our mouths clashing. That sexy, musky scent I'd missed filled my lungs.

"Is it really you?" I studied his face.

The intensity of Steele being with me struck hard, and he was smiling so adorably, sucking in the air like he was inhaling me into him.

One hand against my ass, the other on my back, he pressed me to him tighter. "This is real, angel."

Then we kissed...hard. The kind of kiss that burst across my mind with all the stars from the universe. His tongue pushed into my mouth, forcing his entry, and I opened up, giving him everything he demanded.

I moaned in his arms, having missed him terribly, but his presence brought me something so much more. A piece of humanity, a connection back to Earth in a place where I thought I'd lost everything.

He tasted me, licked my mouth, and growled with hunger. Euphoric waves of arousal flared through me.

When he pulled away, the fog in my mind started to fade, and suddenly, a coldness washed over me as the reality of him being here struck me.

Everything I'd learned about Steele and the queen came rushing forward. How Seven and Ash insisted Steele had once been part of their circle, close to Creed, and worst of all, responsible for killing their queen.

The thoughts left me dizzy with confusion. I had no idea how to feel except overwhelmed.

"W-what..." I couldn't form words at first, and I wriggled out of his arms until my feet kissed the floor. "How did you get here?" I needed to hear the truth from him and not put my own words into his mouth. I deserved the truth from him after all these years. Him being in Wyld was obviously no coincidence.

"I'll tell you everything. The truth of who I am, and why I left Wyld, which you'll find is nothing like the lies I'm sure you've been fed."

I blinked at him, too many questions whirling in my mind. When I parted my mouth, he stole my words with a kiss, then whispered, "But not now. We have to go before it's too late."

The sting of alarm bells rang in my head...something just felt off. I retreated a few steps. "No. You need to tell me now. I'm obviously confused because here I was, thinking you were just human like me, but that isn't the case...is it?" I asked sarcastically. I closed my eyes and took a deep breath, only to open them and see Steele's pained face. "They say you killed the Wyld queen. I..." I sucked in rushed breaths. "Who are you, Steele?"

Hurt-filled resignation crossed his face, and for a moment I was captured in his gaze, the tightness in my chest deepening. I'd allowed myself to have feelings for Steele, and even now with so much mistrust between us, I still craved his smile. I desperately wanted to hear him say that it was a huge misunderstanding.

I didn't want to believe that I'd given my heart to a killer, someone who was the enemy of the monsters who'd been slowly creeping into my heart as well.

My mind raced, and everything inside me hurt because something just told me I was about to be broken. I tried to calm down, knowing I had to get the facts before I did anything rash.

"Blake. There's so much you don't understand. But I'll explain it all to you. I will. But if we stay here, we're both in danger. I didn't kill the queen, I promise, but the person who did, they're still here in Wyld." He reached out for my hand, while I stood stunned and unsure what I was supposed to believe or do next.

Seven

I saw red.

Rage bled through me, and I was charging through the city, my heart pounding in my ears, not even bothering to check where the other monsters ran.

Blake. That was all I thought about. Reaching her and ensuring her safety.

I didn't trust Steele... not after he'd destroyed our kingdom and sliced our queen's head off. It was too much of a coincidence he appeared now, when we found ourselves a potential new substitute for the throne.

What did he want now? To eliminate Blake too?

Who the fuck was I kidding... Blake was so much more than our queen had ever been.

And Steele's death was long overdue.

Burning up with rage, I rushed over the interlinking bridges, not paying attention to the startled stares of the monsters I passed. I leapt madly from one bridge to the next, to reach our tower.

The closer I got to it, the more convinced I was that was where I'd find the asshole.

Everything else around me blurred, and as I leapt up on

the railing of a bridge, readying to catapult myself to the next one, pink hair caught my attention from in the distance.

My heart stopped beating for a moment as terror carved right through me.

I twisted my head to the wide bridge leading right toward the front gates. Lava dripped on either side of the bridge and into the abyss from stone walls. It was a morbid architectural design the queen had insisted on. She wanted anyone who came into our city to immediately feel fearful.

My attention honed in on Blake.

She wasn't alone.

A man in human form had her by the arm, rushing with her away from the tower and along the lava bridge. It had to be Steele. Other monsters outside of our circle rarely took human appearances.

Of course it was him.

Fucking cunt. I roared and sprinted along the railing, feeling nothing but fury. Then I threw myself over to their bridge. I landed on bent knees, sucking in ragged breaths.

Fury rose through me.

Steele snapped around at my thundering footsteps. Our gazes clashed.

At first, I blinked, slightly confused because the man wasn't the Steele I remembered in human form. It threw me off, until I remembered how Steele was a chameleon, just as powerful as Creed, and with that, he carried various abilities.

While the rest of us could take only one human form, Steele had the power to transform into various human guises.

It took me a moment, but I recognized this form of his. We'd seen it in Blake's dreams before we'd kicked him out and taken them over. It was the psychologist she'd been lusting over. This whole time he'd been near her.

That was how he'd slid past our defenses, wasn't it? How

he'd been near Blake without us suspecting a damn thing. We would never have recognized him like this.

Fucking bastard.

His human face twisted into hatred, morphing into his monster form in seconds—dark, hideous face, large head, and his shadows flaring around his body.

He shoved Blake aside with a clawed arm. She stumbled and fell to her ass near the railing, then she saw me and her eyes bulged with terror.

My heart hurt to see her that way.

"Brother," Steele growled, embracing his monstrous form. His grin irritated the hell out of me. We'd been searching for him so long, and of course he'd gotten his claws into our Blake.

Black mist twirled his body, his monstrous form expanding with thicker muscles. His talons and fangs were bared.

I smirked, ready to rip his head off. I needed a damn good fight.

"You're a fool," I snarled. "You should never have stepped foot in Wyld again."

"You have no idea what you're talking about," he snapped. "Be a good dog and fuck off out of here." His head tilted back, unleashing an ungodly war cry carrying his threat.

The others would be here soon enough, but not before I killed him first.

I cut Blake a quick look where she crouched down at the edge of the bridge, her face pale with fear. I'd prefer if she wasn't with us, but at least the bastard hadn't taken her from us just yet. A few moments more, and he would have stolen her.

That notion enraged me, and my blood boiled.

"I'm going to kill you now," I said calmly, then I lunged at him, moving so fast he didn't have time to react.

I slammed into him, my fist thundered into the side of his face. He lost his footing, teetering backward, and I was on him, never relenting with my strikes.

His growls deepened, and my punches flew faster.

Black shadows from Steele's body leapt at me, instantly swarming me, wrapping around me, blinding me.

Just enough of a distraction to catch me off guard for a second.

That was all it took for me to receive a kick to my gut, powerful and strong. Next thing I knew, a punch connected with my chest that sent me flying across the bridge. I slammed right through the railing, stone crumbling behind me, while I precariously landed inches from tumbling to my death.

"You asshole," I shouted, shoving myself to my feet while Steele licked his fangs, glaring at me. "You're making a huge mistake, but if you want to keep playing, I'm game." He beckoned me with a clawed finger. "Blake is mine, and I'm here to collect. I found her first."

Anger flooded me, and I lunged at him once more, this time driving my body upward into the air, heading right for him.

I crashed into him, his legs crumbling beneath him as I grabbed the huge bastard by the throat and tossed him toward the railing. He grabbed hold of the edge and bounced back over like a fucking spider.

Blake was screaming her head off in fear that I'd get hurt, I guessed. She was a sweetheart like that, and I'd show her I was fine in just a few moments.

Steele flew at me, claws extended. The fucker moved fast... too fast because I didn't get out of his way quick enough.

He drove me to the ground, my head smacking on the hard floor. My world danced just long enough for the prick to slash his claws across my face. Sharpness stung over my skull, and I growled, my stomach clenching at the wave of pain.

I bucked and slammed my fists into him. Steele had always been a powerful beast, and before I got the chance to throw him off, his mouth opened, fangs lengthening.

He bit down into my shoulder, tearing flesh.

I yelled, and darkness took over as *he* surged forward.

BLAKE

I screamed.

Stiffening, I curled my knees into my chest, unable to escape the savage battle.

Grunts. Thunderous punches. Bones breaking.

Steele had kept so much from me.

What I'd seen in my dream—him in his monstrous form—was real. He *had* been visiting my dreams, feeding on me too... just as the monsters had done back on Earth.

This whole time, he'd been working in the asylum, hiding from the monsters who hunted him down.

Steele suddenly flew off Seven's body, wrenching me from my thoughts. In seconds, both monsters were on their feet, somehow bigger, scarier—especially Seven. Even the way he stood tall, his head slightly tilted to the side, reminded me of the monster who trapped me in my room and pinned me to the windowpane, forcing me to orgasm.

Steele and Seven charged and they clashed, sickening blows filling my ears.

Tears rolled down my cheeks to see them fighting so savagely.

Their blood splattered everything, skin slashed with teeth and claws. They were going to kill each other. I knew deep in my aching heart that one of them would die today if they didn't stop.

They crashed into the bridge, smashing holes through it, destroying the place.

And I didn't want any of us to fall into the lava pit.

I jolted to my feet, needing to stop them–any way I could.

Just then, Seven slid across the bridge on his back after Steele tossed him. He came to a stop inches from my feet. Blood covered his face and body, and he wasn't exactly getting up either.

My heart strangled me, and I fell to my knees, tears blurring my eyes. "Seven," I cried out, right before a tremendous roar had me flinching.

Lifting my head, I met Steele's darkening stare.

He heaved for breath, his chest rising and falling rapidly, his claws coated in blood...Seven's blood.

"What have you done?"

I doubted he heard me. Not when he growled like a wolf.

Just then, Ash darted past me like a bullet in his monster form, the air buffeting into me, sending me crashing against the bridge's side. He rushed Steele, his claws and those huge horns were all I saw.

Growls boomed around us, their battle vicious. There were no other monsters on the bridges or balconies watching us. It felt as though they were too terrified to even be seen.

Someone suddenly landed feet from Seven's body, as though they'd just fallen out of the sky, and I screamed, rearing back.

It was Creed. He was enormous, veiny muscles pulsing across his monstrous body, and a snarl ripped from his throat. His face twisted with distaste at the fight, but he turned to me first, a softness wiping away the fury. That was when I noticed Tempest rushing in to help Ash.

"Are you hurt?" Creed asked me, drawing my attention to him.

I shook my head. "I'm scared and don't know what's going on."

"Stay with Seven. I need to finish this. Steele will pay for touching you, Blake. I promise you that he'll never touch you again." Then he rushed into battle, the bridge shuddering with each of his powerful steps.

But what if I wanted Steele to touch me again?

The fight was moving too fast for me to follow. Steele's words kept going over in my mind.

The lies I'm sure you've been fed.

My fingers gripped onto Seven's shoulder, shaking him. "Get up, please."

He groaned, his eyes opening lazily. They trained on me, and he smiled. "Hello, beautiful," he groaned.

An ear-piercing snarl had us both turning toward the trio at the end of the bridge. Seven pushed himself to his feet, teetering at first.

I reached out for him. "Maybe you should rest."

He didn't seem to hear me as he shot toward the chaos regardless.

Tilting my head to the fight, I couldn't tell where anyone started or ended, but Tempest had been tossed aside, grasping his side. There was no blood that I could see, so it could be internal damage.

Fuck, how strong was Steele? He'd always been gentle with me, and here he was, facing off with four monsters and he still hadn't fallen.

It didn't take long for Ash to get hurled so hard against the bridge's side that he swung right for the dripping lava wall.

A scream tore from my throat, and I scrambled to my feet in terror. Lava dripped onto one of his horns, sending him flinching backward and shaking his head, then attempting to scrape the fire liquid off with the flick of his hand. He howled with pain.

I rushed over to him, tearing my thin jacket off. "Use this," I called out and threw my clothing.

He snatched it out of the air and frantically wiped his horn, dread all over his face.

The loud crack of bones snapping had me shuddering, and I jerked my attention to Creed slamming Steele to the ground with such viciousness, I cringed.

The next thing I knew, Seven and Ash were leaping to grab onto Steele as Creed wrenched him to his feet by his throat.

I whimpered at seeing Steele like this. I needed to tell Creed not to kill him because things weren't adding up. There had to be more to the story... The Steele I got to know wasn't a killer. He couldn't be.

In a chaotic ambush, they gripped Steele tightly, while he thrust against them, roaring like a wild beast.

They all leveled punches into Steele, doing anything to keep him there.

I cried out. "Stop. Creed, please stop."

I stumbled up on my feet, needing to chase after them. They moved fast as they picked Steele up and began to carry him away.

His head twisted in my direction, and for a brief moment, our gazes met.

Agony. Dread. Fury. They all bled behind his eyes. Along with heartache like he knew this might be his end.

I screamed, chasing after them, holding his gaze until something sharp whacked me right in the back of my head.

My knees gave out instantly, and the darkness came for me.

The last thing I heard was Steele's startled roar at seeing me fall. Then the darkness took me.

Chapter 16

Blake

I woke up to a killer headache–and something tickling my face. I went to brush off my skin in annoyance, only to feel some...scales? Shrieking, I opened my eyes and sat up, screaming even louder when something solid and heavy fell into my lap. I looked down and saw what looked like a giant toad sitting in my lap, at least three sizes bigger than the ones on Earth. Instead of slimy skin, it was covered in scales though, and when it looked up at me with its two bulging eyes, it seemed to smile, revealing two rows of razor-sharp teeth that were dripping what resembled green slime.

My head was spinning as I scrambled to my feet, the frog monster thing falling from my lap into the sand and burying itself underground before I could blink.

Wait a second...

Sand?

What the fuck?

I started trembling as I stared at my surroundings. All I could see in front of me was desert sand as far as the eye could see, extending out under the red sky, nighttime quickly approaching.

How did this happen?

I turned around and gasped when I saw the giant walls that surrounded Wyld at least half a mile in front of me, extending far higher up in the sky than I could ever climb.

I went to take a step towards the wall to see if I could walk there and try to get someone's attention so I could be let back in.

And then the ground began to tremble under my feet.

I heard the sound of sand shifting behind me and I turned, dread building in my chest.

When I turned, I almost wished I hadn't, because as the sand shifted, something enormous and terrifying started to rise up from under the sand.

I was so fucked...

Continue with Book 2 of the Monster and Me Duet on Amazon at books2read.com/monsterandme2

Monster's Obsession

Monster and Me, Book 2

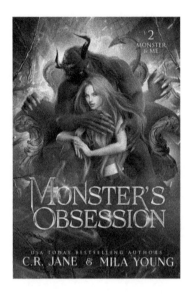

The Monster King wants to play...

The riveting conclusion to the Monster and Me Duet.

Grab your copy today.

Author's Note

This book was so much freaking fun to write. We hadn't created a new fantasy world for awhile and putting together all the details for Wyld and our monsters was an absolute blast. I hope you fall in love with all of these monsters like we have! Just in case you wanted to see what a Gazen actually was that our poor girl is about to face:

Thank You:

A huge thank you to Caitlin and Leah, the best friends and beta readers imaginable. Every time we tell them...oh yeah, this book is due in a day—they come through. And their encouragement and friendship is everything!

Another thank you to Juan for this epic cover. It's so gorgeous I just want to frame it and stare at it all the time.

Jasmine Jordan: With our crazy writing schedules, Jasmine is a godsend. She's willing to take our chapters in all their forms and she's been such a blessing to find!

And to all of you- thank you for letting us continue to do what we love. There are no words to describe what your support means to us.

Wild Moon

Book 1

While you wait for book 2 of the Monster & Me Duet to launch, dive into our Real Wolves Bite series...

I was taught my whole life about the importance of true mates, how when you find that one wolf for you, everything falls into place.

Everyone who taught me that was a liar.

When I found my true mate, happily ever after sure as hell didn't start, but hell definitely began.

I ran away, and now I've been searching for peace for weeks as I drive around the country.

I didn't mean to take the wrong road.

I didn't mean to make it to that small town.

And I didn't mean to meet two men, who set me and my wolf on fire.

But here I am somehow, and peace is the last thing I've found.

And don't forget about the serial killer...

Get your copy of Wild Moon today!

Chapter 1
RUNE

I was cursed.

That had to be it.

I'd come to this conclusion somewhere on the highway, lost in the middle of nowhere, in a strip of land so empty and so flat, it made you feel like you were the only person on the planet. Hours after my car had been broken into while I used the restroom, leaving me with only a twenty-dollar bill to my name.

I'd been driving for weeks...or was it months already? And the only conclusion for why my life had thus far been a giant shit show of the most epic proportions was because I was cursed.

I was perhaps also an idiot.

The sun was falling in the west, and the sky was a kaleidoscope of color. A mixture of pinks and reds that at one point, would have made me shed a tear, back when I had a heart that could still be affected by beautiful things.

Alistair had sucked all the beauty out of my life, twisted and tore at my heart until it was incapable of viewing the world as it once had.

And yet something inside of me, something that was irrevocably tied to him for forever, it still missed him. Despite what he had done, what he'd kept from me. Despite the fact that I'd been told my whole life how wonderful my life was going to be once I found my true mate, and then he promptly destroyed any notions of happily ever after I'd ever dreamed about.

Despite all of that, I still wanted him.

And I always would. Because that's how true mates worked. It was a bond that forced you to need something, even if it would kill you.

Hence why I was thinking that I was cursed.

I dragged myself away from my pity party as the sun finally sank below the horizon. The landscape was changing around me. Jagged rocks were springing up from the land that I'd sworn had been flat as a board just a few minutes ago. Had I been lost in my head for that long? That wouldn't have been a surprise since I'd spent most of the last few weeks stuck in my head. I really needed to pay attention every once in a while though.

The landscape was definitely getting higher and higher, and I could see even steeper peaks up ahead. The road in front of me winded up through them. And now the sun was officially gone, and the stars were peaking their way out in the velvet sky.

Did I mention I was terrified of heights? And not just heights, add in driving and the dark too, and you officially had the trifecta of ridiculous fears that I'd developed over the years.

For a moment, I contemplated pulling over to the side of the road and trying to sleep until the morning. I quickly shook that thought away.

Despite the fact that a part of me wanted to be with Alistair, my true mate, desperately, all the other parts wanted to make sure we never saw that asshole again. The large majority of my parts also wanted to live, and Alistair would kill me after what I'd done. I knew that for a fact.

Taking a deep breath, I continued to drive, and it just kept getting darker and darker.

There were no lights out here, of course there wasn't. Because why put lights in the middle of nowhere? I put my brights on, not giving a fuck. If I was going to drive through a mountain range in the pitch black, you better believe I was going to be able to see while doing it.

Looking in my rearview mirror, I began to freak when I saw headlights approaching. Any time I saw another car, I wondered if it was Alistair, if somehow, he'd found me despite the crazy precautions I'd taken to be hidden from him. Like the way I'd snuck a stash of cash from Alistair's safe and bought a car with it when I was supposed to be grocery shopping. The way I'd used more of that cash to pay for everything I'd done on this road trip from hell. The way I'd gotten rid of my cell phone when I left so there was no way he could track it. The way I'd been wearing an ebony wig twenty-four-seven to try and change my looks.

I breathed a bit easier when I saw it was a Honda Accord. Alistair wouldn't be caught dead in a car that didn't scream money and privilege. While I was all about the practicality and the gas mileage of a Honda, Alistair wouldn't get in one no matter the circumstances, even if it was the only way to catch me.

My breathing increased however as the terrain began to rapidly ascend and I realized I was no longer approaching the mountain, I was going up the motherfucker.

There was a guardrail off to my right, but that didn't calm me down. I was now hyperventilating as I white-knuckled the steering wheel and leaned forward, trying to make sure I stayed right on that white line. If I was on that white line, then I wouldn't go off the edge. Right?

A loud honk had me jumping in my seat, swearing, and swerving the car. I hadn't handled unexpected things with grace over the last few years...but could I really be blamed for that after all that had happened?

I tore my eyes off the white line and glanced in the rearview, only to see that there were now a few cars lined up behind me. The driver behind me seemed to be waving his hands around.

Whoops. A glance at my speedometer showed that I was going about ten miles per hour right now. I highly doubted that was the speed limit, based on the cacophony of angry honks I was beginning to hear.

I rolled down my window, continuing to keep my eyes on that white line since my brain was filled with images of my car tumbling down the side of the mountain and bursting into flames fit for an action movie. I began to wave my arm out the window, trying to get them to go around me. Was there etiquette for this? Besides the obvious move of not driving forty miles under the speed limit.

The car behind me finally got the hint, and it swerved around me, honking loudly and rudely as it did so.

"Jerk," I muttered. The rest of the cars followed their leader, their brittle horns filling the night.

And then finally, it was just me.

Which maybe I hadn't been thinking through, because now that there weren't any other angry drivers to worry about, I was more aware than ever that I was painfully alone.

"What will it be like, Mama? When I find him," I whispered to my mother as she curled up beside me on the bed, a copy of Harry Potter *laying in her lap just as it was every night.*

"He'll make all your dreams come true, baby," she said with a gentle smile. "He'll see all the parts in your heart, and he'll accept them no matter what he finds."

"Why are there different parts in my heart?" I asked, the six-year-old me very confused about the words my mother was saying.

She giggled in that magical way of hers, and I watched entranced at the love I could see in her eyes. Was every mother that wonderful?

"I just mean, sweetheart, when you find him, you'll feel complete," she said sweetly as she brushed a piece of hair out of my eyes.

"Did you feel complete when you met Daddy?" I asked, sadness creeping down my throat at the blurry memory of a man as big as a bear who always smelled like peppermint and those cigarettes he used to smoke constantly as he anxiously paced around the room.

Something in my mother's eyes flickered and changed. There was a look there that I didn't recognize, but which made my little heart uncomfortable because it was so unfamiliar from the gentle looks my mother always gave me.

"Do you promise it will be like that?" I spit out, suddenly desperate for that look in her eyes to go away and for her to give me the reassurance I could always expect from her.

"I promise," she whispered, that look in her gaze fading slowly away.

I settled back into my pillows, ready to hear what Harry, Ron, and Hermoine were up to next, confident that the future was bright because my mother had said so.

Too bad my mother turned out to be a liar.

"Holy shit," I screeched, swerving out of the lane as something black...and furry, sprinted across the dim light of my headlights, startling me out of my journey to the past where I had no business spending time in the middle of the night in the freaking mountains.

"What the hell was that?" I whispered as I slowed down even more and tried to look around.

An even larger furry beast suddenly sprinted in front of my car, and this time, I yanked the steering wheel way too far to try not to hit it.

I screamed as my car went flying past that white line and careened off the embankment, the guardrails nowhere to be found. I went a few feet as I frantically pressed on the brake, those visions of my car tumbling down the mountains suddenly coming true right before my very eyes.

Was this how it ended? A sucktastic life ending with a fall down a mountain in the middle of nowhere.

Only me.

Shrubs and small trees...combined with my braking power, succeeded in slowing down my car, but the pine tree on the edge of the thick forest in front of me succeeded in stopping me completely. I choked on a scream as I hit the tree. The impact sending me flying forward as the airbags burst out of the steering wheel and door. I hadn't hit the tree very fast, but the force of the airbags sent me backwards, my neck whiplashing as it snapped back. The airbags ripped at my skin, burning my forearms, and a noxious plume of gas filled the air.

The silence after the crash was deafening for a long moment. But then a loud buzzing filled my ears as the adrenaline crashed against my veins. I coughed, wearily trying to wave my hand around to clear the air, the enormity of what had happened settling over my skin.

"Fuck," I gasped out. The human mind was truly exceptional. I mean, the fact that it could feel a myriad of emotions all at once as I was now.

Incredible.

"No, no, no," I cried out as I hit at the airbag and steering wheel in front of me.

My head and neck were beginning to hurt the longer I sat there, and a glance at my arms showed me that I did indeed have burns and lacerations from the stupid, fucking airbags.

"Okay, you can figure this out," I coached myself as I quit beating at my steering wheel and turned my attention to unlocking my seatbelt, which judging by the pain I felt in my chest, had definitely stopped me from flying through the windshield.

Small mercies.

After the seatbelt was successfully dismantled, I struggled against the car door, the movement sending agony against my protesting muscles. *This is why you shouldn't live on gas station snacks and fast food for weeks on end*, I thought to myself. *Maybe it wouldn't be so hard to open a small thing like a car door if my muscles actually existed in my arms anymore.*

Success! The car door finally flew open, and I promptly fell out of my seat into the shrubs and rocks that were waiting for me just outside. Apparently, my legs weren't working anymore.

I shivered as I looked around. Somehow, my lights were still working, and the area around me was eerily illuminated.

There was a thick forest just ahead of me. And although I couldn't see anything...it felt like something was watching me.

I shivered again and decided it was best to try and get to the road and see if I could flag someone down for help. Although really, that was probably worse than staying here by the trees. I'd seen the news, I knew the danger of trying to hitchhike, especially out in the middle of nowhere like this. With my luck, I'd get picked up by a mugger or a murderer...or even Alistair. And not to mention those two animals I'd seen...

I groaned and reached back into the car to grab the tiny flashlight from my door that I'd picked up at...you guessed it...a gas station, and then I limped my way back towards the road, which was a seriously difficult task since I'd fallen down a shallow embankment. The roots, rocks, and weeds didn't exactly help. I was not a hiker. I was only a few feet away from the road when a howl ripped through the air. I stopped in my tracks. That thing inside of me that had been there for as long as I could remember perked up at the sound. There was a time that a wolf's howl meant home. A time that I believed my howl would once call out into the night. My mother had promised that it would be a moment I would remember forever.

That was just another one of her lies.

Although I'd once welcomed the howl of a wolf, right now, the sound was a reminder that I was in the wilderness and there was a real possibility that I could be eaten. There weren't any shifters out here, I'd seen the map many times as Alistair tried to plan world domination or whatever it was that he was interested in. Which meant the howl I was hearing was not a good sign.

Fuck, I sighed. I really was cursed. Deciding to proceed with my plan, I finally made it to the roadway, praying the next car that came by didn't contain a psychopath. I'd definitely already had my fair share of those.

I waited.

And I waited.

And I waited some more.

How was it I couldn't get cars off my ass earlier, and here I was, actually wanting cars to be on my ass, and they were nowhere to be seen? Had I taken a wrong turn somehow and stumbled upon a road that no one went down? I squinted at the road, trying to see if it looked like it was in disrepair. I hadn't noticed any out of the ordinary bumps.

"Are you fucking kidding me right now?" I screamed at the night sky, cursing at it for what felt like the millionth time.

Sighing and deciding I was going to just have to walk off this mountain myself, I set off down the dark road.

Weren't the stars supposed to be brighter out here? Where was the freaking moon?

I stumbled over a rock and barely caught myself with my hands. Of course, catching myself meant scraping my palms on the coarse asphalt and dropping my flashlight.

"Shit," I whispered, picking myself up and cradling my hands against me as the pain shot through me.

And there was a wolf howl again.

Perfect.

I'm sure the smell of my bloody palms was going to get me eaten alive.

Wouldn't that just be the most ironic way to go...ever.

I snorted, hysterical laughter threatening to spew from my mouth. I was definitely losing my mind.

Something shifted across the road just then, and I froze, the threat of laughter abruptly coming to a screeching halt.

I picked up my flashlight and began to jog down the road, despite the fact that I knew you were never supposed to run from a predator.

Where were all the fucking cars?

When nothing attacked me from behind, my confidence grew and I started to run faster, despite the fact that my legs were screaming in protest.

I came to a halt when a road that diverted from the main one I'd been running on appeared in front of me just a ways off. I hesitated and tried to squint farther down the main road. I should just stay on this road, right?

The sound of something running down the main road seemingly straight towards me made the decision for me, and I darted down the roadway and quickly realized that it was going downhill rather than uphill as the highway had headed. That was a good sign I thought.

I sighed again as I slowed down to a quick walk, the effects of the crash and my extremely poor diet over the last few weeks doing me in. If I had to run again because something was after me, I was probably going to have to accept it.

Damn those Cool Ranch Doritos.

The air was freezing here. I had on a stained *I Love New Mexico* shirt I'd found in one of my convenience store runs. It was pink, so I knew I had to have it. Alistair had hated pink, banned it from my wardrobe in fact...

Was it going to last forever, this way that my heart would squeeze every time I thought of him? How was it possible to hate someone with every fiber of your being but still feel like you couldn't breathe without them?

I stifled a sob, determined not to cry for him.

"Never again," I whispered to myself, even as his face appeared in my mind as I remembered the way he'd been looking at me right before he ripped my world into a million pieces that had no hope of ever being put back together.

I was so lost in my four hundred and twentieth pity party that it took me a while to notice the lights beginning to pop up in the distance and the enormous wooden sign with the symbol of what looked like a wolf carved above a scrawled 'Welcome to Amarok.'

Amarok? What kind of name was that? And why hadn't I seen this on the map I'd poured over before setting off today?

I pushed myself to go faster, the lights giving me hope, even if I was wary of getting so close to civilization. The places I'd picked had been out in the middle of nowhere. Small inns and motels where drifters and vagabonds passed through, perfect for a girl on the run. Alistair was a big fan of the Four Seasons, so the places I'd picked were, again, perfect for avoiding detection.

Another howl sounded through the night, and I decided that going near people, and hopefully getting help for my car, was a much better outcome than the possibility of getting eaten alive.

I already knew what a wolf's bite felt like, and it wasn't an experience I wanted to repeat...

Get your copy of Wild Moon today!

Books by C.R. Jane

www.crjanebooks.com

The Sounds of Us Contemporary Series (complete series)

Remember Us This Way

Remember You This Way

Remember Me This Way

Broken Hearts Academy Series: A Bully Romance (complete duet)

Heartbreak Prince

Heartbreak Lover

Ruining Dahlia (Contemporary Mafia Standalone)

Ruining Dahlia

The Fated Wings Series (Paranormal series)

First Impressions

Forgotten Specters

The Fallen One (a Fated Wings Novella)

Forbidden Queens

Frightful Beginnings (a Fated Wings Short Story)

Faded Realms

Faithless Dreams

Fabled Kingdoms

Fated Wings 8

The Rock God (a Fated Wings Novella)

The Darkest Curse Series

Forget Me

Lost Passions

Hades Redemption Series

The Darkest Lover

The Darkest Kingdom

Monster & Me Duet Co-write with Mila Young

Monster's Temptation

Monster's Obsession

Academy of Souls Co-write with Mila Young (complete series)

School of Broken Souls

School of Broken Hearts

School of Broken Dreams

School of Broken Wings

Fallen World Series Co-write with Mila Young (complete series)

Bound

Broken

Betrayed

Belong

Thief of Hearts Co-write with Mila Young (complete series)

Darkest Destiny

Stolen Destiny

Broken Destiny

Sweet Destiny

Kingdom of Wolves Co-write with Mila Young

Wild Moon

Wild Heart

Wild Girl

Wild Love

Wild Soul

Stupid Boys Series Co-write with Rebecca Royce

Stupid Boys

Dumb Girl

Crazy Love

Breathe Me Duet Co-write with Ivy Fox (complete)

Breathe Me

Breathe You

Rich Demons of Darkwood Series Co-write with May Dawson

Make Me Lie

Make Me Beg

Make Me Wild

Books By Mila Young

www.milayoungbooks.com

Savage

Lost Wolf

Broken Wolf

Fated Wolf

Shadowlands

Shadowlands Sector, One

Shadowlands Sector, Two

Shadowlands Sector, Three

Shadows & Wolves Complete Collection

Chosen Vampire Slayer

Night Kissed

Moon Kissed

Blood Kissed

Monster & Me Duet Co-write with C.R. Jane

Monster's Temptation

Monster's Obsession

The Alpha-Hole Duet

Real Alphas Bite

Kingdom of Wolves

Wild Moon

Wild Heart

Wild Girl

Wild Love

Wild Soul

Winter's Thorn

To Seduce A Fae

To Tame A Fae

To Claim A Fae

Shadow Hunters Series

Boxed Set 1

Sin Demons

Playing With Hellfire

Hell In A Handbasket

All Shot To Hell

To Hell And Back

When Hell Freezes Over

Hell On Earth

Snowball's Chance In Hell

Kings of Eden

At the Mercy of Monsters

Kings of Eden

Stolen Paradise

Ruthless Lies

Wicked Heat Series

Wicked Heat #1

Wicked Heat #2

Wicked Heat #3

Elemental Series

Taking Breath #1

Taking Breath #2

Gods and Monsters

Apollo Is Mine

Poseidon Is Mine

Ares Is Mine

Hades Is Mine

Sin Demons Co-write with Harper A. Brooks

Playing With Hellfire

Hell In A Handbasket

All Shot To Hell

To Hell And Back

When Hell Freezes Over

Hell On Earth

Haven Realm Series

Hunted (Little Red Riding Hood Retelling)

Cursed (Beauty and the Beast Retelling)

Entangled (Rapunzel Retelling)

Princess of Frost (Snow Queen)

Thief of Hearts Series Co-write with C.R. Jane

Siren Condemned

Siren Sacrificed

Siren Awakened

Broken Souls Series Co-write with C.R. Jane

School of Broken Souls

School of Broken Hearts

School of Broken Dreams

School of Broken Wings

Fallen World Series Co-write with C.R. Jane

Bound

Broken

Betrayed

Belong

Beautiful Beasts Academy

Manicures and Mayhem

Diamonds and Demons

Hexes and Hounds

Secrets and Shadows

Passions and Protectors

Ancients and Anarchy

Subscribe to Mila Young's Newsletter to receive exclusive content, latest updates, and giveaways. Join here.

About C.R. Jane

A Texas girl living in Utah now, I'm a wife, mother, lawyer, and now author. My stories have been floating around in my head for years, and it has been a relief to finally get them down on paper. I'm a huge Dallas Cowboys fan and I primarily listen to Taylor Swift and hip hop...don't lie and say you don't too.

My love of reading started probably when I was three and it only made sense that I would start to create my own worlds since I was always getting lost in others'.

I like heroines who have to grow in order to become badasses, happy endings, and swoon-worthy, devoted, (and hot) male characters. If this sounds like you, I'm pretty sure we'll be friends.

I'm so glad to have you on my team...check out the links below for ways to hang out with me and more of my books you can read!

Visit my **Facebook** page to get updates.

Visit my **Amazon Author** page.

Visit my Website.

Sign up for my newsletter to stay updated on new releases, find out random facts about me, and get access to different points of view from my characters.

About Mila Young

Find all Mila young books at
www.milayoungbooks.com

Best-selling author, Mila Young tackles everything with the zeal and bravado of the fairytale heroes she grew up reading about. She slays monsters, real and imaginary, like there's no tomorrow. By day she rocks a keyboard as a marketing extraordinaire. At night she battles with her mighty pen-sword, creating fairytale retellings, and sexy ever after tales. In her spare time, she loves pretending she's a mighty warrior, walks on the beach with her dogs, cuddling up with her cats, and devouring every fantasy tale she can get her pinkies on.

Ready to read more and more from Mila Young?
www.subscribepage.com/milayoung

Join Mila's **Wicked Readers group** for exclusive content, latest news, and giveaway.
www.facebook.com/groups/milayoungwickedreaders

For more information...
milayoungauthor@gmail.com

Lightning Source UK Ltd.
Milton Keynes UK
UKHW010924100622
404197UK00002B/238